40 Hours and an Unwritten Rule

40 Hours and an Unwritten Rule: The Diary of a ~~Nigger~~ ~~Negro~~ ~~Colored~~ ~~Black~~ African-American Woman

Kim Williams

butterfly ink publishing

BUTTERFLY INK PUBLISHING
P.O. Box 56874
Sherman Oaks, CA 91413
www.butterflyinkpublishing.com

Copyright © 2004 by Kim Williams
Illustrations by D'Mario McDonald and Tawanna McDonald
Edited by Chandra Sparks Taylor

All rights reserved, including the right of reproduction in whole or in part in any form.

ISBN: 0-9745423-2-6
LCCN: 2003097379

Printed and bound in the United States of America

Although situations are loosely based on actual events, this is a work of fiction. Names and characters are the product of the author's imagination or used fictitiously, and any resemblance to actual persons, living or dead, is entirely coincidental.

To Gran and Aunt Margaret

acknowledgments

First, lots and lots of thanks to my dream buddy then and my dream buddy now. Marilyn and Allana, without your support I would have never found the words or realized the possibility. Marilyn, thank you for helping me build and nurture my dream. And Allana, thank you for helping me to rediscover it.

Tawanna, thanks for your generous heart and creative mind.

Thanks to all of you (and you know who you are) who took the time to read and share your thoughts and ideas. And a special thanks to Mama, Jackie, Angela, Ber, Janice, Al, D'Mario, Joe and Sharron.

kim
-Life is a journey, not a destination-

The BIRTH of a ~~Nigger~~

see opportunity
ve in reincarnation
perceived me to h
th to ugly babies
ring of the past
in my own skin

PERSONAL PROPERTY

birth of a nigger
October 26

Dear Diary,

Have you ever seen a baby so ugly that for a brief second you allow yourself to feel sorry for the union that conspired to produce its adverse little life? Who could create such a thing? Was it lust, love, jealousy, revenge? You begin to wonder if something so unattractive will ever get a fair chance to blossom into a flower worth picking. How many times will he be teased and criticized in our narcissistic society for nothing more than his existence? Will he ever be able to cover his unappealing features with a foundation of acceptance? Will he be rejected because of the unforgettable impression that he will leave on others? Can he ever experience unconditional love by someone other than his own ugly kind and reproduce another generation, and will that one be as ugly as the last? Will he ever reawaken into an acceptable existence that society wouldn't perceive as being as ugly as the first?

    Then again, Mama never believed in reincarnation.

She feels that when you die, that's it. You're dead. You either go to heaven or hell. No in between. No coming back as a bird or a tree. No second chances. Just heaven or hell. So, naturally I grew up believing the same thing. I guess we really have no choice. From birth we usually just develop the same beliefs and habits as our parents since it's from them that we've learn how to live. We don't second-guess our embedded points of view and challenge everything that we once thought of as truth until we start observing original thoughts and unfamiliar ways of life later.

Do you believe in reincarnation? If you would've asked me that question a few years ago, my answer would have been no. And if you asked me why, I would have answered, "because my Mama said so." But if you ask me today, I will say, "I'm living proof."

From what I was told, there wasn't a dark cloud in the sky the day of my first birth. It was a clear, bright sunny afternoon with great opportunity for anything to happen. That's why Mama used to call me her "little Racey rainbow." (I don't know why she even bothered to name me Raceyneisha. No one has ever called me by that awful, ethnic name, thank God). You see, in the days leading up to my first arrival, there was a terrible storm that carried nonstop hard rain and breezy winds. And then there was me, an unlimited spectrum of beauty, innocence, serenity, and possibility. Mama has always believed that I didn't have an excruciating entrance because God was making up for the disastrous storm He had created days before.

But some births are filled with unexpected complications and unbearable pain that even an epidural can't cure. I guess you can say my second birth was somewhat like that. Although it seems like a lifetime ago, it has only been four years. The morning that I was delivered onto the pale, conservative campus of my new environment,

birth of a nigger

the city was filled with low clouds and dark skies. And the upcoming storm had no plans to welcome any past promises that I represented. It was hard to comprehend because the previous summer afternoon had been shining with anticipation of a new start. But I guess some things are just unpredictable.

I always knew that I didn't want to go to a black college. I had been around black people all of my life. Growing up, I had no white neighbors, and I had only two white classmates. What were their names? Oh, Sarah and Tina. Yeah, and no one ever really thought of them as being white; they were just a really, really light version of us. But when it came to "real" white people, I remember I always used to hear: "Watch them." "They don't care about nobody but themselves." "They need Jesus." "You can't trust them." "It's just a matter of time before they show their true colors." "They think they're better than us."

Knowing what I know now, I can't believe that I actually accepted these slanted beliefs all of those years. But before I went away to college, everything that I had perceived the majority to be was based on what I thought was my family's factual opinions. I never even thought to question them 'cause I didn't think it was possible for Mama to ever be wrong. Even though she was wrong about carrots. I ate carrots all of those years thinking they were giving me good vision. I even had carrot cake for my birthday every year. And then at thirteen, it happened: carrots proved Mama wrong. I needed glasses. I haven't eaten a carrot since.

At the beginning of my freshman year, I fought to ignore my family and prove them wrong. My positive attitude overshadowed all of the uncomfortable feelings of being the only one. I answered the silly questions and tolerated the constant stares. I was willing to do whatever it took to earn my place in the real world. Unsurprisingly, it didn't take long for me to begin to foster my new extended family's dreams and adopt their acceptable habits. And yet there were still those who didn't welcome me into the family. Instead of supporting and focusing on my growth, they concentrated on conceiving yet another birth for the campus to raise. You see, my new relatives were the types who depended on aid from society and used past government checks as a reason to continue producing ugly babies. I know that you've seen at least one of them: boy, girl, nigger. Yeah, like I said earlier, some are pretty repulsive. For them to have seen me as anything more than an ugly baby the moment I met them would have taken a drug that appears to be impossible to manufacture. So, some people keep doing it their natural way—giving birth to ugly babies regardless of the difficult process that follows and the lasting pain that lingers.

I remember on my first day, my roommate shared that I was the first black person she had ever met. It didn't really bother me because I was in a somewhat similar situation. The difference between us was that I was willing too ignore the perceptions that were given to me by my family. Karen Hoffman, on the other hand, wasn't open to getting to know me as an individual; she was only interested in seeing me as "one of them." We had many disagreements about whether or not all black people were stupid and violent. It didn't help her argument that I was in the honors program and she could barely spell three-letter words. But throughout the year, her stupid ass continued to debate all of African-Americans' flaws in society.

The frivolous campus disputes didn't help either. There was the protest against the Black History Month celebration since there wasn't a white history month, a heated debate on whether or not minority faculty would devalue the university's reputation, and a claim that minority financial aid programs were prejudice against white students. After the first year, I was with my family. I couldn't stand white people. I was angry and frustrated at their perceptions and at myself for allowing them to get to me. I even thought about accepting Farrakhan's beliefs.

But according to society's definition of potential, the odds were against me the moment I left home. Growing up in a single-parent apartment, we didn't have much. But I never knew we were poor. I always thought it was common to struggle for what you need and wish for things you want. It didn't really matter because I never wanted material things anyway. I always dreamt for the skill to compete in the real world. And that's why I ignored boys, fashion, and all that other teenage crap. I concentrated and worked my butt off through school to get to where I am today. My goal was simply to become qualified to play in the game so that's what I did. At seventeen, I abandoned home for college. And after college, I left Texas and started my new life here in Los Angeles.

I just grew so tired of hearing everyone complain about sitting on the sidelines waiting for their turn to play. That's why I decided to just walk on the field and force everyone to play with me by grabbing the ball. I joined a sorority and other professional organizations that would give me credentials. I not only worked full-time, but I interned every semester to sharpen my skills. And after four years of training, it worked. So I've decided to throw all of my ill feelings toward "them" out the window and start over. Tomorrow is the first day of my career, a fresh start, but when it comes down to it, no one really cares about who's actually playing in the game, right? Everyone has the same goal: to not only win a championship but to walk away as MVP.

My crazy family, however, believes that my game theory could be proven in a perfect world but since that doesn't exist, my progressive philosophy, a phrase coined by Uncle Sonny, is just a bunch of wishful thinking.

Family's Game Plan

1. Mama: The makeup of players is crucial to their exclusive game and because of our strong abilities to grasp and excel in anything that we attempt, they'll never invite us to play.

2. Uncle Sonny: There's a bigger conspiracy to keep us from even trying out.

3. Gran: There's always an ulterior motive if by some miracle we even make second string.

4. Cousin Ray-Ray: We just need to play our "own damn games" instead of always trying to learn their single, complex one.

    Yep, that's the optimistic family. Now, I wouldn't say that they're prejudiced or anything—well, not all of them anyway. Hmm, I just don't know about Uncle Sonny; I've witnessed some of his prejudiced tendencies. But I think most of them are just a little overly cautious. So, in an ironic way, I guess there are perceptions on both sides, huh?
    But isn't it funny how our negative opinions of them never seem as powerful as their negative perceptions of

birth of a nigger

us? Somehow, ours are even sometimes acceptable or so insignificant that it doesn't seem to matter what we think. Come on, can anyone really blame us for still being a tad bit suspicious?

Think about it, have any of our perceptions, however negative or inaccurate, ever influenced their lifestyle or livelihood? I mean really, truly affected their everyday life? But what about some of the names we've been called:

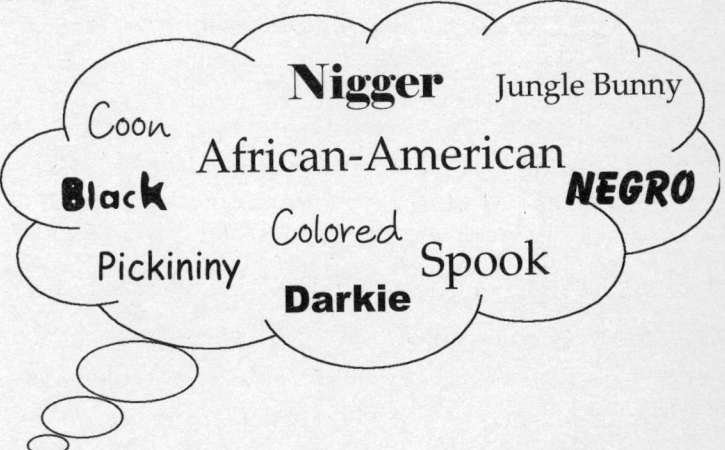

These names are the exact reason why I can't watch those old movies, especially the pre-Civil War ones. You can even forget *Roots* if it's not February. If we're answering "yes, sir" to anybody then it's "no, ma'am" for me to sit through them and hear some of the derogatory names that have been created for our differences and their egos. And it never fails, after watching one of those movies, the littlest thing just sets me off and makes me want to avenge every life that has been taken away by those ignorant, malicious names. I get enraged at all of the years that these names have effortlessly nurtured disrespect, intimidation, limitation, and exclusion to their prosperous life.

And it sucks that the only reason that these names

even came about was because of difference. It seems that people always associate different with being something bad or not equal to the same. I remember I used to hate my pretty hazel eyes and dusty sandy hair. Growing up, it seemed that everything about me from my red caramel skin to the little brown freckles on my pointy nose was a mistake even though people were always telling me how they loved how everything complemented my unique red shade. But instead of seeing it as a positive thing, I gazed at the thoughts: What's wrong with me? Why did God make me this way? How can I change to be like everybody else?

I don't remember exactly when it happened, but one morning I looked in the mirror and didn't mind staring my differences in the face. I no longer wished for Snow White's perfect beauty or a Black Nubian Queen's distinctive features. I just desired to be me, my different-looking self. I wonder what's taking society so long to wake up to its morning of acceptance.

But how do we really expect those memorable names to just disappear with the other scary nightmares that we can't remember once we're awake? It's just not that easy. I'm not for holding grudges 'cause if that were the case, I would be sitting at home with Cousin Ray-Ray justifying why I'm playing some illegal shit. Maybe we just need to really think about this. We still have negative opinions about white people's differences. So, how can we expect them to not have negative perceptions about ours?

That's why I have a good feeling about this new job. I'm taking the first step toward change. After taking a year off to regroup, I'm now ready to live to my full potential. And after a preppy, white college training, I'm now qualified to play with the best of them and disprove their negative perceptions. I'm finally an adult in their world. With my determination and passion, this has to be a guaranteed win, right? I know how to blend in instead of sticking out in their minds. I've mastered their language and personality. I've learned how to tolerate all of their differences. Of course, I will always have my overly cautious family's tactics in the back of my head, but I'm ready to keep them there and prove their old-fashioned theories wrong with my one optimistic hypothesis: It's not like that anymore, especially in the real world. I'm now stepping onto an equal playing field.

Don't worry, I'm not going in thinking that even though I have an advantage, I don't have to play hard because of my past defeat of surviving a majority white environment. I'm just going to show everybody that I have a strategy as well as the moves to tackle my latest list.

> 1. See Opportunity
> 2. Taste Acceptance
> 3. Hear Comfort
> 4. Touch Life
> 5. Breathe Success

I can't remember where I came up with these lists. Probably Oprah. My shero! Actually, if it weren't for Oprah, I would've never started writing you these letters again. Before college, I was always writing something. I was even yearbook editor my senior year of high school.

But freshman year, my honors college professor snatched the pen right out of my gullible hand. She claimed that I was a horrible writer with no style. With me being new in her world, I thought that she had to be right. I still remember the day that redirected my life from strong-willed to fear. The next morning, I changed my major from print journalism to public relations and my thought of becoming a writer was erased from my dreams. This is actually the first thing that I've written since that day because now I know that it wasn't me, although sometimes, I'm still a little critical of my thoughts. Funny, how one can influence others to do things they would have never thought about doing, huh?

But I'm almost positive that I got the list thing from Oprah. It just sounds like something that she would have on her show: "Today on *Oprah*, the power of lists!" Now I'm obsessed with lists. And they really work too! I don't know what it is but for some reason when I write it down, it feels like the words gain an identity within the ink instead of just imagination drifting from my desires. So now, I can't seem to stop numbering my many thoughts.

Well, it's getting late and I have a big day tomorrow. So, I'm just gonna put a little faith in my new team, whoever they are, to help me experience yet another victory. Hell, I'm even striving for MVP. So tomorrow morning, when I sprint onto that artificial turf, I'm going to show everybody (even Cousin Ray-Ray). I'm gonna be ready to play ball.

there's no place like home

October 27

Dear Diary,

I'm the only one. I knew my chances weren't great, but damn, I thought that maybe there had to be a small possibility. Come on, we're everywhere now! We're no longer limited to just service-type roles. We're running corporations and building dreams. Is this normal? Whatever happened to affirmative action? You would think that there should at least be two of us.

But there was nobody there today, just me. I guess I should get used to it, huh? After all, I'm in the "real world" now, the true American workplace. And once again, I feel like the only living soul in an abandoned haunted house.

40 Hours and an Unwritten Rule

The moment I walked through the doors of my new home today, I immediately scanned the spacious room for a pair of warm, brown eyes but I only felt the cold, blue ones staring. So, once again, I knew that I would never be comfortable enough to really feel at home. Instead of a charismatic condo, it was just another studio apartment with a floor plan that I couldn't redecorate because of the placement of walls and restriction of space. I would never be able to kick off my shoes and walk around barefoot or take off my coat and enjoy the household warmth. From this day forward, it would be eight, uncomfortable hours sitting on the couch as a guest with my shoes and jacket on.

As I was walking across the room, I immediately had to search for all of the crap such as the frustrating thoughts, the mind conversations, and the lonely feeling that I had abandoned in college because all of the clutter had crowded my last apartment. I thought they would clash with my new place but unfortunately it was the same color scheme. But it wasn't hard to get them back because I had memorized them like an Earth, Wind, and Fire song and had only stopped singing them a year ago.

"Excuse me?"

"I disagree . . ."

". . . Not all of us are like that."

After I recaptured the necessary defenses and reset the positive attitude, I was ready. Ready to represent. Ready for change. Ready to succeed. Ready for progress. Ready to make new friends. Ready to pick battles. Ready to educate. Ready to fight. Ready to experience all the same bullshit that I had experienced before but this time I was ready to overcome it and win.

"Welcome, we're like a family here."

birth of a nigger

Those were the words I heard all morning as people passed by my new cubicle. I was trying to look past the words and behind the smiles to feel if my new relatives were inviting me into their family or letting me know that there was no room for a distant cousin. I mean, some looked sincere. But others wore the same fake smiles that greeted me my freshman year of college.

"Thanks. I'm just trying to remember everyone's names."

What else could I say? "I'm so happy to intrude on your bland family, and I look forward to adding a little spice in your world." I think not. You know, sometimes you just have to go with the flow. You have no choice but to adapt to the gated conservative community. You can't play your music too loud because there are some of them who still haven't jumped on the wagon of hip-hop. You have to watch what you say and how you say it for those who will rate intelligence on spoken words. And you must raise your tolerance of what is acceptable and what's not.

At the same time, you still have to be optimistic. What if everyone is genuinely happy to get to know the new cousin? And what if when they look at you they see no difference than they do when they talk to their sister? And what if it doesn't matter that you're not in the immediate family because family is family and there's one love for everyone? It could happen.

Okay, so maybe it can't happen for everybody. So, after being trained for an hour on the simple system of the office, I jumped into my new routine that Mama warned me I would not only have to learn, but kick ass performing. And of course, after an hour, I mastered it.

Who knew it could be done? Especially by a cousin.

That's what I perceived to be going through the minds of my supervisor, Kathy Roberts, and our coworker, Lisa

Klein, as they approached my cubicle. It wasn't the first time I had met doubt and surprise before being drilled about my capabilities. I had experienced similar qualms as the only black student in the honors program in college. Kathy had decided that Lisa had to see it with her own eyes because it had taken her three weeks to even understand the basics, which didn't surprise me after having a conversation with Lisa. She had gotten the job not because of her superb qualifications but because her uncle and the CEO were old college friends.

I was doing my thing, going through the system like I had been doing it for years because it was simple as hell. I mean, anyone with common sense could master it. And there they were ... looking over my shoulder, waiting for me to fuck up so they wouldn't feel so stupid.

As Lisa continued to breathe her doubt on my shoulders, she was shocked. "Wow, Racey! You must have done this before, huh?"

"No, this is my first time."

"But have you ever worked with this kind of system?" Kathy asked.

"No, first time." I smiled.

"Did you go to school for this?" Lisa thought that there had to be an explanation for this.

"No, in college, I was actually a journalism major with a concentration in public relations."

In unison, they replied, "Oooooooh, you went to college."

Oh, you're one of those!

"And you majored in public relations?" Lisa asked.
"You must be smart."

Yeah, smarter than your dumb butt if it took you three weeks to understand this.

"Where did you graduate? Or did you finish?" Lisa asked.

"Yeah, actually I was in the honors program."

See, I did that on purpose. I purposely didn't answer Lisa's question about me graduating. I wanted to say, "Actually I graduated with honors." But you have to keep them guessing. Gran always said, "No matter what you do, don't tell them all your business." But don't worry, they will find a way to ask it again.

"Wow! Did you have a scholarship?" Lisa continued.

Because that's the only way we go to college.

"Actually, I did."

Again in unison, they replied, "Ooooooh!" As in Oh, that explains everything.

Okay, that was my first incident. I knew I couldn't go through my first day with nothing. Mama had warned me that this could happen so I wasn't totally surprised. But a little part of me really wanted Mama to be wrong.

After lunch, half the day was over and so far (except for the college incident), so good. I had accepted my new life and decided to make the best of it and fit into my new address. The afternoon was filled with all the corporate crap that everyone has to do on their first day. I completed my human resources forms and checked the box that confirmed that they were the good guys and were doing their best to diversify. Surprisingly, I got through the safety video, the corporate video, and the diversity video without falling asleep. After orientation, I received my house key: an ID card with my new work address printed next to my photo. It was official. The moving trucks were gone, the neighbors had introduced themselves, and I had a room filled with unopened boxes of all the things that

40 Hours and an Unwritten Rule

had been sitting in storage since my college graduation. I was at home.

Afterward, I walked around the rest of the building to meet everyone and get a full tour of my new neighborhood. It wasn't until the end of the tour that I knew all hope wasn't loss. We stopped on the south side of the building. "Brotha! Sista! Mama! Daddy!" There was my nuclear family handling the mail, office supplies, trash, and anything else that the family upstairs didn't want to deal with daily.

"Hey," I yelled.

"Do you guys know one another?" Kathy asked.

Although I had never met them, we all knew one another like we had grown up playing hide-and-seek together. Of course, my cousin Kathy couldn't understand.

"No," I answered.

As she struggled to remember names, she introduced me to my birth family. Suddenly, I didn't feel alone anymore. Even though I had to take a trip to the south side to see them, I was excited because at least they were there. And I knew that they would understand when I needed to come visit.

Why is it that black people always speak to one another like they know one another even though they're strangers?

That was the question Kathy wanted to ask but wouldn't dare because she wouldn't understand, and for that reason wouldn't care about my answer. So she continued to wonder, and that was fine with me.

Remember when you were scared to go to a public rest room by yourself? You just wanted someone to hold your little hand and walk you into the strange stall that lacked the warmth you were used to from your bathroom at home. And at a certain point it wasn't necessarily that you were unable to hop onto the toilet and just pee by yourself. (Well, in my case, squat because Mama would've killed me if she caught me actually sitting on the seat.) It was more that you were just used to a familiar face guiding you to strange places and being there while you took care of your business.

But one day, I remember Mama telling me that I was a big girl and it was time to go by myself. She then warned me that if I peed on myself, I was going to get a whippin' because I knew better. Eventually, I ignored my fears and just did it: peed alone.

Well, today, I went by myself, and something about it was just as frightening as the first time. Somehow I couldn't remember the motivational speech that I wrote last night. I could only recall another first time four years ago. Even though I had chosen change over comfort, I was scared to death of the challenges that change would give me. And no matter how many honors classes I excelled in or how much discipline it took to finish a four-year program in three, I still felt that I was just an infant in their adult world. But I thought it would be different today because I had proven my growth in their fantasy world. Why is it so hard for them to accept us for nothing less than them? I had traded layaway for Gap. I expanded my vocabulary. I even started watching *Friends*, thinking I could relate to them better. But it never seems to be enough. Today, I was asking myself the same questions that I did on my first day of college.

1. Why am I here?
2. Am I only here because I'm black?
3. What do they think of me?
4. How can I fit into their world?

5. What is it going to take for me to be comfortable?
6. Are Ray-Ray and them right?

I thought those days were over. I was sure that with a college degree and my broadened experience, I could camouflage my way into their minds as being the same. But instead, I feel like I still have to prove myself to their historical minds; I have to go through the birthing years all over again. My intelligence is still challenged. My race, regardless of how many championships we've won, is still sprinting to be accepted in a competition that doesn't seem to have a finish line.

I don't know. Maybe I'm overreacting. What if Kathy and Lisa were just genuinely being nosy and had no other hidden agenda than to satisfy their own curiosity. This was my first day. I couldn't get upset at every little thing. I might as well join my bitter family, which I refuse to do. I'm on my own now and that means figuring things out for myself. Figuring them out. Figuring out this place they call the real world. Figuring out how to go by myself and learning how to take care of my business on my own.

good morning!

October 29

Dear Diary,

Is it just me or does everyone think that it's unacceptable to be treated like anything less than a human being? I understand the tired political games, but you have to draw a fuckin' line somewhere. It doesn't have to be a straight one every time. Sometimes you have to ignore professionalism and forget trying to use a black pen and an accurate ruler. These are the times where it's not about the color of the pen or the measurement of the divider; it's only about right and wrong.

"Good morning."
As he walked away, I was puzzled. I was sure he heard me speak because he looked me dead in the eyes

and my mouth isn't that far away where he couldn't have seen it moving. But I'm a fair person. I'm willing to give everyone the benefit of the doubt. Anyway, he must have a lot on his mind. After all, he is the CEO. When I was first introduced to Brenden Mayer during my interview three weeks ago, he came across as a conceited, conservative jerk with very little respect for anyone who couldn't provide him with something he didn't already have. And from the looks of things, he seemed to have everything.

But I'm all for giving people the benefit of the doubt. Maybe he was contemplating a huge decision that would affect his six hundred employees. I couldn't hold that against him because I would be affected as well. And I was here to make his job easier. I know how some decisions can cloud your mind and consume your life at certain moments. I hadn't been able to focus while trying to decide if I wanted Chinese or Italian for lunch.

A day later . . .

"Good morning."

As he walked away this time, I was pissed. Now I know he heard me because I made sure to speak a little louder, and he not only looked me in the face but also responded with his infamous "Does she know who I am?" smirk. He had graced me with the same slight smile with his nose in the air when we were first introduced. But while he was asking me, he should have been asking himself, "Do you know that she is a black woman who demands respect from everybody and she doesn't give a damn who you are or what you do?" But it's okay, he soon will learn.

So, the following morning, he slowly walked by my cubicle waiting for me to greet his rude ass. Well, let's just say that he's still waiting. You don't have to tell me three times. I'm not that slow! My self-respect wasn't about to let someone throw it a curve ball and strike out—even if it meant having to walk to all four bases instead of hitting a home run.

The next day I watched him pass every cubicle before mine and not acknowledge the workers without a title before their names. Who did he think he was (besides the CEO)? Forget elevated positions and job titles, what about the person? Everyone deserves a certain degree of respect. Does he speak to his mama? I know that she isn't a vice president. What about his wife? She's just a housewife with no job, no kids, a live-in maid, and a personal trainer. What's wrong with people? And I'm not only talking about the jackass in question. What about the common people in the office? Why don't they demand respect? Why do they continue to speak to him day after day? Had they fallen in love with that devious smirk that he gave them in return? Were they hearing voices that I couldn't hear? Did they not notice that he wasn't speaking back? So, I decided to investigate.

I knew that Peter Ross in Accounting would have all of the answers. He was the wealthy office mole. His parents were filthy rich, and he was only working to prove to his father that he was independent. But anytime he needed money, his independence always became secondary to his desires. On my first day he offered to give me the lowdown of the place over lunch; therefore, I felt that he would truthfully answer any question I asked.

"Does Brenden speak to you?" I asked.

"No, he doesn't talk to anyone who isn't a director or above," he answered.

"Hmm, I wonder why people continue to speak to him?"

I knew the pathetic answer to this enlightening question but I decided to confirm my suspicion.

"You have to speak to him. He's the CEO."

Hmm, it's funny that they felt that way. I would think that the same applies in reverse: He has to speak to me. I'm a person. But I guess I was the only one who felt that way.

A few days later . . .

Today began like any other. I booted up my computer and checked my personal e-mail; prepared my instant oatmeal in the company's filthy microwave—What! I'm not cleaning up after these people. I am not the maid—checked my in-box; and prepared to face another day at the office. That's when it happened, the moment that was unimaginable by my untitled coworkers. But I knew it would happen eventually. Everyone craves attention, especially CEOs.

It started off like all of the other days. He exited the elevator with all of his insecurities mistaken for arrogance that he brought to work every day. He walked down the row of cubicles being greeted by every person occupying them and responded with his infamous disrespectful smirk.

And then it was my turn. I made sure to look up from what I was doing like I had every morning since the second time. He was a few feet from my cubicle. Our unrelenting eyes met as he began to pass my area. What? I wasn't about to speak to his butt—I didn't care if he was the President of the United States. He still has to respect me. He better recognize my strong, single, black mother upbringing!

"Good morning."

Well, it's about time! Even though it was a whisper so low that even Superman would have struggled to hear it, those were his first words to me and it would do—for the moment.

"Good morning, Brenden."

Who knew that my first words in this place would be silence?

conversation about nothing

November 9

Dear Diary,

Do some people just like to hear themselves talk or do they really think they have something to contribute to every conversation? It's like they're addicted to their words. Maybe it's just the way I was raised, but I've always thought that you were only suppose to speak when you have something important to say. Otherwise, just keep your stupid, irrelevant thoughts to yourself.

"Have you been to that new Cuban restaurant on Third?"
"Yeah, I hear that it's pretty good."

Peter was telling me about the latest restaurant scene in the area before Brandi Harris in Human Resources interrupted.

"Excuse me, guys. I just wanted to introduce myself. We talked on the phone before you started. I'm Brandi Harris in HR."

"Oh, hello. I'm Racey Thomas. Nice to finally meet you," I said.

Well, that was nice of her, to go out of way to welcome me to the family. See, I knew they weren't all bad.

"We were just talking about restaurants in the area."

"Oh, I forgot about that new place on Vineland. It's supposed to have great sushi," Peter remembered.

"Speaking of restaurants, I have this great story."

We both stopped and stared at Brandi's eagerness to impress the "new girl." I knew that this was going to be worse than getting through three rolls of a coworker's nondescriptive vacation pictures. She was ready to drive at minimum speed down a dirt road that we both didn't care to visit, but we had no choice because we were both trapped in the backseat tightly fastened in our seat belts with the child safety locks activated. The only way loose was to wait for the airbags to explode, which I knew would only be a matter of time. I hate road trips.

"I have this good friend, Robert. He's African-American."

As she said, "African-American" she began searching for my approval. What? Did she want a cookie? She not only knew another black person, but they were close friends. Should that impress me?

"We were having dinner one night with one of our mutual friends Brian and his new girlfriend who neither of us had met. So, Robert and I were standing outside the restaurant waiting for them to arrive."

Yeah, yeah, yeah. Can you get to the point?

"And mind you, this was a classy place. Brian has expensive taste because his father is this big producer."

As she said "big producer," she began searching for my jealousy because she knew someone who knew someone. What? Did she want a cupcake? My cousin's boyfriend's sister is married to the cousin of Danny Glover.

"So, they finally drove up and Jenna got out of the car. She's this snobby princess who obviously didn't grow up in a diverse environment like I did because when she got out of the car, she gave Robert her car key and told him not to drive the Benz too fast. Can you believe that?"

Actually, I can't believe that you thought this story was relevant to a discussion of restaurants in the area.

"Some people are so ignorant!" she exclaimed.

My thoughts exactly.

"Of course, Robert was fuming. But I could tell he was too angry to handle the situation. So, I had to step in . . ."

Isn't it funny how well we can read people? I guess with all the broken promises of things, such as land and freedom, we were forced to develop a skill of detecting the sincere ones. But sometimes we don't have to work hard because the phony ones make it so easy. Did she think that I was so stupid that I couldn't detect her plan of trying to disguise herself as the savior of the north who was going to help me free myself of the stereotypes of the office? Did she really think I needed her help unpacking my baggage and decorating my new home? She was trying to create harmony and didn't even know the basic principles of feng shui. So, how was she going to help me balance the water of my ancestors and the metal of my past with the wood of my potential and earth of my aspirations with the fire of my future?

"So, I jumped in because Robert is like my best friend."

As she said "jumped in," she began searching for my gratitude. What? Did she want a brownie? Was I suppose to be so impressed by her colorblind ethics that I would recognize her friendship potential?

"I mean, the nerve of some people. I told her that just because Robert is an African-American male doesn't mean that he couldn't dine at an expensive restaurant."

Yeah, you told her. Maybe you should be the spokesperson for all African-Americans who have been mistaken for someone else.

"She felt so stupid."

Are we there yet?

"She spent the rest of the night so uncomfortable because Robert is very educated. He graduated from Howard. I'm sure you've heard of it. She was totally embarrassed that he was totally smarter than her. I tell you, some people."

If I really wanted to confuse her, I would've said, "Actually, I've never heard of Howard. Where is it?" But I didn't want to get stranded with another long, boring-ass story about the history of black colleges, so I replied, "Yeah, some people."

"Hey, maybe we should get together. You know, go see a movie or something," she suggested.

Only if you promise not to tell me another story.

"Uh, sure. That sounds great."

"Yeah, you know everybody's not that cool around here. If you know what I mean, right, Peter?"

"Uh, sure," Peter said.

I swear, some people just need attention. Some people need to belong. Why do they always have to fit in no mat-

birth of a nigger

ter what the situation? And why do they think that any long-ass, irrelevant story that connects them to our side in any kind of way, shape, or form is always the perfect size? If I would have interrupted her and Peter's "restaurants in the area" conversation with a story about the time I broke up an argument between a rude waitress and disgruntled customer at Denny's, would she have found that story relevant? And I actually saved the blond waitress from getting her butt whipped by an entire table.

Has anyone told them that it's okay to be the minority sometimes? Hell, we've been doing it since we were captured from our majority land. Or maybe they're afraid of the guilt that would consume them if they experienced being the "only one" sometimes. I don't know the reason but I do know that if I hear another "I can sympathize with you because I've been a witness to injustice" story to prove that "I can relate and am willing to stand up for any prejudice even when I'm not the target so let's be friends" story that has nothing to do with nothing I'm going to scream.

"Which reminds me of another story."

AAAARRRRRRGGGHHHHHH.

I don't know why I get so upset sometimes. I guess it's the family's genes. I wonder if I didn't have the perceptions in the back of my head, would I have enjoyed the story? Maybe I had missed out on a genuinely good story. Maybe I'm being too whiny. But I'm trying. I want to give these people the benefit of the doubt, but sometimes it's so hard. Why do they always have to speak in goo-gahs when they first talk to us to pacify their comfort level? Don't they know that we can relate and build friendships on grown-up stories? I wanted to tell her, "No matter how many amusing stories you try to entertain me with, you will never fully understand my screams and fusses with everyday life, so stop trying." But I knew my outburst would be as understandable as any other agitated baby trying to explain why it was upset, so I just continued to stare and smile and wonder if it was just me.

have you ever seen chinatown?

November 16

Dear Diary,

Expectations. Everyone has them. Whether it's presuming that it will rain because the sky is gray or assuming that if you work hard, you'll be rewarded, we all expect certain things to happen. But then there are those expectations that society has created and ran so many times that we recognize them at the opening credits. Most of the time, even though we know the ending, we sit through it because the popcorn and Whoppers make it tolerable. But then there are those times when it's so bad that we have no other choice but to walk out.

"Come on, let's ask Shiho. I know she'll know."

"Oh, yeah! I forgot about her," Miranda remembered.

As Miranda Schwartz and Amy Baker passed my cubicle to find Shiho Robinson who was standing three cubicles down, I was wondering what would Shiho know. Peter had told me she was going to school for interior design so maybe it was a design question about furniture or decorating.

"Hey, Shiho."

"Hey guys, what's going on?"

"We were trying to figure out how to get to Chinatown," Amy said.

No, they didn't.

First of all, Shiho is a Japanese-American with little to no ties to her Japanese culture. A pro-American family who hadn't seen the importance of teaching her any other culture other than American adopted her when she was a baby. Their idea of preserving her culture was giving her a Japanese name. But Miranda and Amy didn't know the difference. They just put everyone in the one group, Chinatown.

If it were me, I wouldn't tell them even if I did know.

"I don't know. I've never been."

"What do you mean you've never been?" asked a shocked Miranda.

"What's in Chinatown?" Shiho wanted to know.

"Uh, we thought you would know."

Yeah, and everyone thought that Eddie Murphy would never make a bad movie.

"Sorry, I don't know."

But Amy wasn't ready to give up. "Do you know anyone who can give us directions?"

"Yeah, like any of your friends?" Miranda asked.

"No, I don't think so."

"Oh, okay. Well, see you later," Amy said.

"Maybe you should look on-line," Shiho suggested.

Suddenly, a light bulb went off in Miranda's head. "Oh yeah, we didn't think about that!"

Yeah, there are a lot of things you didn't think about. Like why would Shiho know how to get to Chinatown?

It's amazing how we're never approached with the political and current event questions, but we're the first person they think of when they need to know how to get to "that" side of town or the name of a non-white celebrity.

Later in the day (yeah, two in one day) . . .

"I'm sure you'll know," Paige Anderson said as she approached my cubicle.

"Know what?"

"What's the name of Snoop's new song? We couldn't think of it at lunch."

"I don't know. I don't listen to rap music."

"What do you mean you don't listen to rap?" Paige asked.

What she meant to say was, "How can you not listen to rap? I mean, you're black. And how can you not know Snoop's new song. I mean, he's black."

I don't understand. Paige and I clicked the moment we were introduced two weeks ago. We had a lot in common because we had similar goals. In the short two weeks, we had also spent a lot of time getting to know each other. So how could she mistake my Banana Republic cashmere with FUBU cotton? Why are we all looked at as the same? Why can't we grow from stereotypes? Why can't they free their enslaved minds to see us as individuals and not as offsprings of the past? This feels like college all over again.

"I'm not into rap."

"Well, what kind of music do you listen to?" she asked.

"Mostly R&B and jazz."

"Oh, I thought everybody listened to rap."

What she meant to say was, "I thought all black people listened to rap."

"Not me," I replied.

She walked away surprised at the twist in the last scene. She was not only confused, but she was frustrated because she thought I had confused her on purpose. I just didn't want to tell her. Why? Did I not like her? Had she done something to me and was unaware of what she had done? Or maybe I was just being difficult. Maybe she needed to give me one chance. Maybe she had missed the dialogue at the beginning that explained the ending. So she decided to go through it one more time.

"So do you know who Snoop is?" she questioned as she returned to my cubicle.

What is this, third fuckin' degree?

I was becoming a little annoyed. "Yeah, why?"

"I was just wondering because you said that you didn't listen to rap."

Ah-hah! She thought she had me. How did I know Snoop if I didn't listen to his music?

"I still don't listen to rap. I know a lot of rappers by their name but I couldn't tell you every song that they've recorded because I'm not a fan of rap music."

"So you know what song I'm talking about?" she pressured.

"No, not really. I didn't even know he had a new song."

"Maybe you just need to hear it and then I know you'll know what I'm talking about."

"Probably not."

So this sequel was just as boring and predictable as the first conversation. Same plot, same characters, same setting, but this time there was going to be a different ending.

"Well, what about . . ."

I couldn't take anymore. "I'm sorry, I have a meeting."

"Oh, okay."

"But if you find out the name of the song, let me know so I can listen to it. It must be really good since you're trying to find the name."

As I was walking to the elevator, I sensed that this wasn't the ending she was expecting. She wanted the same predictable story that the critics would call Oscar-worthy. But there was nothing else left for me to see, and I personally wasn't enjoying the story. I was expecting a shorter conversation with better dialogue and action.

But I know my expectations were different from hers. She was presuming that all of us knew every single detail about each other. She was expecting me to entertain her with an answer to any "black" question she asked. She was assuming that we all enjoyed the same type of entertainment because, unlike them, we didn't have our own personal taste. We just liked everything spicy. And they wonder why we can't relate to them sometimes.

but i'm always right!

December 19

Dear Diary,

Why do people deny their ignorance? I mean, we've all been wrong at one time in our lives. But it seems that some of "them" refuse to believe that those times ever happen in our presence. I don't care what the topic of conversation is, they will try to convince you that their two cents is worth more than your dollar thought. Why do they think that they know everything? Why do some think they are qualified to answer every question regardless of the subject? Just because we got a late start in the reading game does not mean we haven't caught up. The tortoise proved that when he won the race.

Kathy had procrastinated and decided to start a six-month-long project today, three days before it was due, even though her boss, Adam Levy, had assigned it to her before I had even started working here. And of course, Kathy blamed the short staff as the reason why she was so far behind because she could never take the blame for anything, especially in front of Adam. But I don't know what gave her the impression that I would not only work for free on Sunday, but that I cared enough to come in on my personal time to help cover her lazy ass.

"Maybe we can finish this Sunday," Kathy suggested.

"Oh, I can't. I have plans."

"Oh. What are you doing?" she asked.

Not that it's any of your business, but "I'm going to a Malcolm X exhibit." I really was.

"Oh, where?"

"Some place downtown."

"What are they going to showcase?" she asked.

"It's like a tribute to his life. You know, artwork, photographs, speeches, things like that."

"That sounds interesting. He was great. I loved his Washington speech."

I can see how she would get Martin and Malcolm mixed up—they look so much alike.

"What speech?"

"You know, the famous one, the March on Washington speech," she replied.

"That wasn't Malcolm. That was Martin Luther King, Jr."

Hopefully the little bell went off in her head and she quickly realized her mistake. I mean, who doesn't know that Martin gave the "I Have A Dream" speech? I would think that Martin would have been covered in the single paragraph, black history section of her high school history book.

"Are you sure?" she asked.

That's just like asking a Baptist preacher if God is real. I'm one hundred percent positive!

"Yeah. Positive."

"Uh, I could have sworn that it was Malcolm," she insisted.

How is this white woman going to argue with me about such an important milestone in black history? Does she not realize that I'm black?

"No. It was Martin."

"For some reason, I remember reading about Malcolm X and his speech. Are you sure that he didn't speak another time at Washington?"

Oh, so now she was trying to turn it around from "the" speech to "a" speech in Washington.

It never fails. They always refuse to surrender their errors. When they see that there's no way to win the battle, they always make the war about something slightly different.

"Oh, I thought we were talking about the 'I Have a Dream' speech," I said.

"Oh no! That was Martin Luther King. I was talking about another speech."

Sure, you were!

"What other speech?" I asked.

"Hmm, I can't remember. But you know what I'm talking about I'm sure. What college did you go to again?"

Ah-hah! I told you she was going to ask again. But remember, keep them guessing . . .

"No, I don't know which one you're talking about," I answered.

"Maybe you'll see it at the exhibit. I'm sure it will

be there. But we really need to stop chatting and get this done since you can't work Sunday. Also, remind me next week to get you started on another project that we need to finish."

It never fails. When they know that you know that they're wrong, they always have to put you back in your place. Did she really think that I was going to remind her to give me another bullshit project that she was going to create to show me that she was the boss? But how could she not know? And why couldn't she admit her mistake? In order to protect her flawed intelligence, she was attempting to teach me how to read my past and write a new history. But she didn't realize that I already could not only read my complex history, but I could also decipher the difficult words of her flawless ego. I wasn't the one who needed to be taught. She's the one who needed a lesson in history but she would never admit it.

let's do lunch

January 7

Dear Diary,

Do the women in my office think I'm stupid? Do they not realize that I'm now allowed to question their answers and answer their questions? That means that I'm going to disagree when I feel that something is wrong. I'm going to ask questions when I don't understand certain actions. We no longer have to sit back and let them dictate what we do and how we do it. Didn't they get the memo? We are free. We're now creating our own menus and have been cooking to please our own tastes. And if they don't like it, they can find somewhere else to eat.

"Okay, that'll be, uh, twenty dollars a piece."
What? Wait a minute. I had a small cup of chicken

noodle soup at six dollars and a glass of water at zero dollars. How in the hell does that equal twenty? The waiter wasn't that good!

"Can I see the check for a minute?" I asked.

"Yeah, but we always just split it. It's easier, and we don't have to figure out the math," Lisa replied.

I don't know whether it was laziness or manipulation. What did they mean by figuring out the math? It's just addition and division. There's no complicated formulas or lengthy theorems involved. Had they not figured out that I didn't order twenty dollars worth of food? Had it not occurred to them that afternoon margaritas and a full-course lunch totaled more than a cup of soup and was valued at more than twenty dollars? And I thought that this was going to be a welcoming lunch.

Initially, I was excited when Lisa asked me to join her and the popular office group for lunch today. Lisa was the designated leader because of her connection with Brenden. So in the minds of Amy Baker, Miranda Schwartz, and Diane Sanders, if Lisa liked me, then they were open to the idea of socializing with me. So I thought that maybe I was finally going to blend in and not be seen as the "different" employee. I was still trying to find my place in my new environment so I hadn't complained about them dragging me to this eclectic restaurant that had the nerve to mess up chicken noodle. I was trying to develop relationships and not stand out as the "militant black girl." But sometimes they make it so hard.

As they were throwing their twenty-dollar bills on the table . . .

"Wait a minute, guys I only had an appetizer."

They were as dumbfounded as the plantation owners hearing the news of the slaves' freedom. They didn't know what to do. If I wasn't forced to obey them, then how were they going to teach me to do what they wanted

birth of a nigger

me to do? They had been doing it this way since the first time they started having lunch together a few years ago. This was their way of life. How could I rock such a sturdy boat?

"Yeah, but it's just easier if we do it this way. That way we don't look silly with calculators," Lisa said.

Well, if you need a calculator, then you're something else besides silly.

This is just something that would never happen with a black group. There are a few things that we are willing to swallow, but being ripped off was too chunky to even chew. We would never say just split it when it came to a difference of a couple of drinks and a meal. If it meant a little extra work to figure it out then it was well worth it. If it meant pulling out a calculator for the more complex calculations, then it's "Does anybody have a calculator?" There was no way in hell that we would allow someone to cheat us. Fair is fair! Right is right! And wrong is just unacceptable!

"Oh, I have to pass out my thank-you cards for Christmas. I don't want the executives to think I didn't like their gifts," Miranda remembered, "Did you guys do yours yet?"

Now that's a first for me. I have never heard of giving a thank-you card for a Christmas gift.

"Wait a minute. We're short. Did I calculate that right?" Lisa asked.

Damn right, you're short because I only put in eight dollars.

"Did everyone put in twenty?" Miranda asked.

I tried to tell y'all the first time and you didn't want to hear me so I'm just going to sit here and be quiet.

"Okay, it looks like we need more money, " Lisa demanded.

It's funny how you can add now.

As she said "money" she looked over at me. She better act like she know even if she doesn't. I wish she would say something to me about putting in more money. Just because they were paying for my labor now didn't mean that they were going to tell me where to spend it. I returned her look right in the eyes with a cold stare. I think she felt the chill because she soon began searching for a warmer pair of eyes.

Well, I guess there goes any future lunch invites. Oh, well, you can't win them all . . . I tried . . . I really thought I was going to indulge in their world today. Eat what they eat. Drink what they drink. But there was no way that I was going to pay what they demanded to be considered a part of them. So I went back to work hungry. I was starving to be treated as an equal but I would starve to death before I would tolerate being treated like a fool.

~~1. See Opportunity~~
2. Taste Acceptance
3. Hear Comfort
4. Touch Life
5. Breathe Success

birth of a nigger

January 16

Dear Diary,

Well, some things never change. I really thought that this was going to be easy. What more could I have done to prepare myself? I guess it doesn't matter how grown you think you are, they always find a way to make you feel like you were just born into their world. The day that I arrived, my coworkers, like my college family, gave birth to a reincarnated nigger in my likeness. Before me, I'm not sure how many times other nigger perceptions had been reborn in my new household, but it seems that it's revived every time an offspring of the original hideous newborn enters a majority environment. You would think some form of present-day contraceptive would've been discovered by now to prevent such repeat accidents in our overpopulated society. But I guess some people enjoy the process of screwing and manipulating to produce the astonishing result that eventually proves that beauty is in the eye of the beholder.

For some reason, I thought that it was going to be different with me. After meeting me and seeing that I wasn't who they perceived me to be, I thought my new family wouldn't go through the stages of watching a nigger birth develop into a negro child, grow into a colored adolescent, settle into a black adult, and rest as an African-American senior. But some people have bared so many perceptions, that maybe it's easier to just push another one out of their close-minded wombs.

Maybe this is what life is really about. There are no words to be spoken, no actions to be performed, or no prayers to be answered; nothing can stop the birth of ugly babies. They will continue to be born as long as people continue to be addicted to associating the labels of the past with the faces of the present.

So why do I want to be like them anyway? I would have to give up so much of me to think like them, and I'm not sure it's worth it anymore. A few months ago, I thought I had no other choice. That's why I went through the trouble of trying to prove that I wasn't different. I allowed them to put me in their playpen and teach me the basic building blocks of the working world. I laughed at their unfunny stories and smiled at their intolerable behavior. But I realize that my foundation won't allow me to be like them, no matter how much I've tried over the years. And I really don't want to anymore, but do I have a choice? Somehow I have to find a way to grow in my own skin instead of allowing myself to get comfortable in theirs. But sometimes it's so hard.

negro childhood

January 17

Dear Diary,

Yeah, those were the good old days... Now, I'm not saying that every single day was filled with treasured moments. But you have to admit, most of them were as enjoyable as my first time at the circus. I remember my favorite act being the acrobats. I would close my eyes while watching them enjoy their freedom, and envision flying to a place that would embrace that moment forever. I can still feel their freedom. Yeah, those were good times. What happened to living being simple? When I was a kid, everything was all about fun, not winning or titles. I constantly indulged in the freedom of bliss. No worries. No cares. Just living. I was able to develop my likes and dislikes, determine my strengths and weakness, and build my personality and dreams on my own. I could dream big back then. And I had no doubts to block the growth of them; therefore, I was forever watering my thoughts.

But now it seems like I'm living for others and even

though I have the freedom to develop, my growth is still enslaved. My choices are limited and my actions are dictated. How can I just live to enjoy instead of living to survive? How do you grow in stifled minds? How can I gain total independence? You know if I could do it all over again, I would have enjoyed life more back then. I wish that I could do it all over again. I wish that I would have taken my time instead of rushing. I wish that I could be free again.

i know you're not going to sing that song!

January 26

Dear Diary,

Why can't they get their own words? All the words that they have claimed ownership of over the years and yet they steal ours every time. But isn't it ironic that the same words they steal are the same ones that continue to stereotype us as being inferior? However, when they use them, they're "connecting" and being cool.

I wish that we could patent our words, you know, make them "black words", only to be spoken and interpreted by black people. Let's face it, some words just don't sound right when they are sang out of tune by an ignorant tongue.

As soon as I entered the kitchen's stage right, I knew I was going to regret being so thirsty that I couldn't have waited a few more minutes to finally quench it. But there was no turning back. Before I saw Amy, Miranda, and Diane standing around conversing, I envisioned the tenor note coming from the dramatic mezzo-soprano chorus. Pick another song! You're not going to hit the cabaletta! Not all of us can sing a rousing opera that can make the hairs on your arm stand! But what could I do? I decided to just get my drink and waltz out like I had strolled in a minute before. But they had different plans. They were determined to turn their trio into a quartet, because I was the only one who could successfully belt out the powerful aria.

"What up, girl?" Amy sang.

Wait! You can't start yet—the lights haven't even dimmed.

"Just getting a Coke."

"How are you liking it so far, girlfriend?" Diane screamed.

"Everything's going good so far. I'm still trying to get the hang of things."

And then Miranda felt the need to include me in their rehearsal. "We were just talking about working out."

"Yeah, do you belong to a gym?" Amy asked.

"Yeah, The Sports Center."

"Oooo, they have some fiiiine brothers over there. I would feel weird working out there," Miranda yelled.

Wrong note! Remember you're a soprano, you can't sing the bass part.

And it's brotha, bro-THA.

"Um, yeah, I guess there are some nice-looking guys.

But usually I take classes so I don't really go in the weight room."

"If I was a member I would be all up in the weight room every day," Diane proclaimed.

"Yeah, girl, you need to hook us up with some guest passes," Amy chanted.

Why is intermission taking so long to get here?

"Yeah, I would fo' sure be getting my groove on up in there," Diane said.

"I know! When we go, I have to make sure that I'm extra cute," Miranda agreed.

You're not following the script.

"But you know what I love to do?"

Is that a rhetorical question?

Of course, I didn't respond to Amy because I was afraid she was going to try and translate the Verdi opera and lose the emotional melody that the original language captured. But you couldn't tell her that because she thought she was "down." Every time she opened her mouth she craved a voice as beautiful as Leontyne. The other members of the chorus were struggling to understand the foreign language so they began to sing.

"What, girl?" Diane asked.

"I know it's ghetto . . ."Amy started.

Stop! Remember I'm the lead! You guys are backup! You're only supposed to sing the chorus!

And can a white person even be ghetto?

". . . but sometimes on my way home from the gym I love to stop at Popeyes for a spicy two-piece and eat it while I read my *Fitness* magazine. It's so good."

Stop singing! You're ruining the story! What happened to the melody?

And when did it become ghetto to eat fried chicken?

Diane was amused. "That's so funny! I think we all have a little ghetto in us. Don't you think, Racey?"

Oh, so now that you've ruined the climax, you want me to give the heart-pounding conclusion?

They all anxiously waited to hear if I had a voice that was worthy of the lead lyric soprano. I had watched all of them commit suicide. I couldn't save this group. They were trying to create riveting drama, but instead they kept belting out tuneless love songs that made you want to fall out of love.

So now they were ready for me to create a deeply moving, beautiful tone that complemented the emotional story, the exotic sets and costumes, and the astounding orchestra. What could I do? I had no other choice but to exit stage left. I couldn't let them destroy the history of such brilliant, emotional music. And I couldn't allow them to ignore the years of collaborations of astonishing composers and gifted librettists. I would not participate in their vicious plot to steal our creative and original style. So, I took a sip of my Coke and belted out the dazzling cadenza.

"I don't know."

As I was walking back to my desk, I began to smell the roses that were being thrown my way. And I heard the audience cheer, Brava! Brava! Go'n girl.

but i don't want to be your friend

January 29

Dear Diary,

Isn't it funny how people are thrown together strictly out of circumstance? I love my black people. I really do but sometimes you just can't relate to all of them. But for some reason it seems that we have no choice but to get to know one another.

It's not that I think I'm better than my family in the basement but I just can't find anything in common with them, besides our kinship. After talking to them a few times, I quickly realized that they were more like the distant uncle and cousins who you only see at family reunions. I wouldn't even strike up a conversation with some of them at the Laundromat because we would never spin on the same cycle. But it doesn't matter if one is gentle and the other is permanent press. We have just been thrown together in the normal cycle to save quarters.

It had been more than a week since I had been downstairs so I decided to take a break to see the folks on the south side. As the elevator opened, I saw the "other one" on the opposite side of the door. She was on vacation the week I started so I didn't know that I wasn't the only sista but later I discovered that I was still alone. She was cordial enough to say hello but that was about it. For some reason, she was trying so hard to fit into the majority group that she had lost all the weight that the rest of us carried on our shoulders. I guess she felt that she would be tempted to indulge if she socialized with me, so she didn't.

"Hello."

"Good morning."

That was it. She had already put her head into the papers that she was holding so she appeared occupied before she had finished the "morning." That was fine with me. It's not like we had the same eating habits. She was on the no-carb diet. And even though I had been watching my figure, there are just some things that I refuse to give up. I crave the breads of my past and the starches of my future. I was proud of my curves!

It was weird. Even though she had managed to get down to a size zero, the elevator still felt a bit lighter when she got off at her floor. But that was alright. I was on my way down to see the "real" people. The people in the mailroom liked to eat and they could care less about fitting into someone else's pants. That's why you gotta love them.

As soon as the doors to the elevator opened, Sean

Jackson greeted me with another one of his sorry pick-up lines.

"So, um, you know, um . . . When we go hook up?"

"Are you serious?" I asked.

Please say no, please, please . . .

"Fo' real though, when can I get yo' number?" he pressured.

"Uh, I have a boyfriend."

Whew! Saved by the "boyfriend" line. Okay, so I don't have a boyfriend and I should leave my options open, but can you really see me with this guy? Don't get me wrong, he's not bad on the eyes or anything. But can we take out the cornrows, invest in some clothes other than jerseys and baggy jeans, and develop a little tact?

"Does that really matter?" he asked.

See what I mean? He's one of those guys.

Not only was he the campaign manager for Phat Farm, he had no concept of my dreams or how to make them come true. The only thing he knew was a minimum-wage paycheck every week that supported his Phat Farm addiction. Don't get me wrong, I will give him some points because I know he has other options, but I still couldn't feel him like that. I had abandoned his lifestyle a long time ago and had discovered that other lifestyles were possible. And I had no desire to move backward. I kept walking as if I was in a hurry so he could abort his mission but he still had his mind on the attack.

"You like to play hard to get, huh?"

Why is it so hard for you to get that I'm not interested?

I was almost to the door of the mailroom. I knew that he wouldn't follow me in with his game in front of his running mates, so I pretended not to hear his screaming voice from the other end of the hallway, but once I entered the mailroom . . .

"Hey! I was just thinking about you. I'm on the guest list to Club Milk Chocolate tonight. You wanna come?"

See what I mean when I say nothing in common?

Although Keisha Grant was on this ridiculous mission to find a husband at a club, she was still decent company at work. I was three years older so I gave her the benefit of the doubt and blamed her immature ghetto ways on being nineteen. For that reason, I couldn't share my worries or thoughts with her because she would never understand; however, she always borrowed my ear to solve her problems.

"It's Tuesday. I have to work tomorrow," I answered.

"Girl, I do too. But Deon is probably going to be there."

Oh, another one? I know I'm going to regret asking but . . .

"Who's Deon?"

"Oh, he's just some trifling guy I met at Club Hershey last weekend. But I need a new sponsor."

Couple of questions:

1. *Why do you need a sponsor?*
2. *And if you "need" one, do you really want a trifling one?*

"What happened to Deshawn?"

"Oh, the sex was good and all but I can't deal with the baby mama drama. You know what I mean!"

No, I actually don't.

"No. I think I'm going to have to pass tonight."

negro childhood

"See, that's why you don't have a man."

Like I would really find a "real" one in a club.

"If you say so."

"That's okay, I think I can get us on the list for Friday."

"Oh, okay. Let me know."

Yeah, like I'm really going. How many times do I have to tell Keisha that I don't go to clubs, especially ones with chocolate references?

"I'll call you tonight."

Did I give her my number?

"Do you have my number?"

"Yeah, girl. Remember that time you gave it to me?"

Why did I give her my number?

"Oh, ok, I'll talk to you later."

"Hey, let me holla at you for a minute."

Darren Wright aka Mr. Sean John had made his way from the recycling bin sorter to the mailroom lounge. His platform was better than Phat Farm's ghetto plan, but let's face it, they're all dogs. He was the supervisor of the recycling department so he was a little over minimum wage and had benefits but he also had six kids by five different women so after child support and his tennis shoe addiction he was right along with Phat Farm. But he wanted something more; he had a decent platform. He had just enrolled at the community college. However, my plan still didn't include stepmother duty.

"Uh, you know I have to get back to my desk. I just came down to drop something off."

"It won't even take a second."

One—your time's up.

"What?"

"So, when are you going to let me take you out?"

"Uh, I have a boyfriend."

Let's see if it will work this time.

"You can bring him too. I just want to get to know you better."

Oh, well, maybe I need to get another line.

"I don't think he would like that."

"You know, you have some pretty eyes."

"Thank you."

"So, um, maybe I can be your friend."

But I don't want to be your friend!

"I already have enough friends."

"Oh, so what are you trying to say?"

You got to be kidding me?

"I have to go."

"Okay, that's cool, that's cool. We'll talk later."

As I was walking back upstairs to my neck of the woods (and I was actually glad for once to live there), I started to think, *Is it just me?* But then I couldn't see how it could be just me. I mean, I want to believe that other people like me exist. You know, middle-class African-Americans who had careers and aren't funding any clothing campaign except a few charitable donations to Banana Republic or Gap. Where were the black people who were proud of all the greatness that's involved in our culture? There had to be black women who could care less about getting their "chocolate" on at any club or nightspot. And there had to be African-Americans who didn't crave anything but blackness. And where were the sistas whose dreams were more than finding a sponsor to give them a lifestyle while they gave up their style in return? What about finding a partner, a mate, a friend? Was it just me?

As the elevator doors opened, Gary Johnson walked

out, returning to his home in the basement. He was the exception of the other folks. A little older than all of us, he made a decent living that supported his family. He wasn't trying to create a scandal or influence a vote. He was also a realist. He knew that he didn't have to try and pull me to his side to coerce my vote. He understood that we were related by color but that we didn't have to automatically relate to each other and become instant best friends. We were coworkers and didn't have to force anything more.

"Hey, how's it going?" he asked.
"Fine. How are you?"
"Fine. See you later."
"Okay, bye." I waved.
"Bye."

I feel like I'm on a divided playground. I remember as a child, for some reason, I had a respected place with both the popular and unpopular kids. With that unique position came the ongoing choice of deciding which group to play with, even though the unpopular kids always played better. It was never really an easy decision. Do you play with the outsiders and risk alienation from the cool group? Or do you resort to acting foolish and ignore the outsiders for the sake of acceptance? And why do you care what anybody thinks anyway? Yep, this was when peer pressure introduced itself to me and it's still pressuring me today with the same shit.

Back then my resolution was to divide my time between both groups without the other really discovering my betrayal. And since it worked then, I figured it should work now. I don't know why I still feel guilty about my choices, but I do. After striving to be like the cool kids, I've grown away from being the person I really am. It's like my arrogant thoughts believe that somehow I'm better than the people on the south side and if I'm spotted being too friendly then everything I've worked so hard for will be in vain; the cool kids will ban me with the outsiders. But deep in my heart somewhere, I know that I'm no better—hell, we're family. And somewhere in my mind, I know that I can't turn my back on my family. I wonder if my absurd feelings are a part of the consequences of trying to fit into the world upstairs. They're starting to influence my perceptions without my consent. I'm confused. Which side do I choose?

i heard it through the cubicle

February 4

Dear Diary,

Why are the people at work so nosy? They're always searching for a scoop and are always prepared to do whatever it takes to get their story. Well, at least they attempt to be credible journalists. It's a different story when it comes to black folks. We're okay with reporting tabloid journalism. But even though you appreciate their accuracy, you still get tired of all of their investigative reporting. Especially when you're being investigated.

"Yes, I would like to make a doctor's appointment... Actually I would like to get in as soon as possible... Oh,

I need my well-woman exam. And I would also like to have blood work done . . . That works . . . Okay, see you then . . . Bye."

I don't know whether she was working on a deadline by trying to get her story on the five o'clock news or if she was just a thorough reporter, but Lisa wasted no time pressuring me for an exclusive. Even after the lunch incident, she had remained interested in getting closer to me because, as she put it, she loved learning about different cultures. It hadn't even been five minutes before she made her way over to my cubicle.

"Are you are okay?" she asked.

She looked as sincere as a hunter waiting for his prey to make that one costly mistake.

"Yeah, everything's fine. Why?"

"Oh, I just overheard you talking to your doctor. And I just wanted to make sure everything's okay."

You mean besides your nose?

"Yeah, I was just making an appointment."

"You reminded me that I need to make one. Don't you just hate those things?" she asked.

"Yeah, I guess."

"Where do you go?"

"Um, this female doctor in the Medical Plaza."

"How long have you been going to her?"

What is this, Twenty Questions?

"This is my first time."

"Oh, yeah, now that you have a job with insurance you don't have to go to a free clinic."

What the hell? Black people have insurance too.

"I actually had insurance before this job."

"Oh. So, um, why are you getting blood work done?"

It's really none of your business, so I'm going to play dumb.

Even though I heard the question the first time, I replied, "What?"

"You said that you were getting blood work done."

"When did I say that?"

"You know, when you were on the phone."

I hate pushy reporters.

I decided to continue playing dumb. "When?"

"Just a few minutes ago," she confirmed.

"Oh, were you listening to my conversation?"

"Um, it's kinda easy since we're in cubicles, you know. I wasn't trying or anything."

Like hell you weren't!

"Oh yeah. They make it impossible for anyone to have a private conversation, huh?"

"Yeah, don't you just hate that?"

Do you really want to know what I hate?

"Yeah, you say one thing and then you have everybody in your business."

That everybody would be you.

"Yeah, it sucks, doesn't it?"

"Yeah, it really does."

I think she got the idea because that was the last question she asked. I don't know whether she was trying to break another scandal or was just doing a feature, but I wasn't about to supply her ass with any more information. She didn't care about my health. It didn't matter if I was dying from a terminal disease or if I was just trying to find out my blood type. But I knew her angle—she was just there to get her story. Sure, she was pretending to befriend the poor victim of circumstance but at the end of the day, she was going to get off her high horse and remove her hood, revealing her true color. She would then set fire to whatever friendship and trust she pretended to develop and watch it burn up right in front of my eyes as she reported my business around the office.

mmmm, that smells good!

February 9

Dear Diary,

Have you ever wanted something so bad that you can taste it? The single thought of good soul food sometimes will trigger that desire. Tender, meaty oxtails; juicy mustard greens; sweet candied yams; spicy finger-lickin' barbecue; cheesy baked macaroni and cheese; golden-fried catfish; mouthwatering hot-water corn bread; warm, melt-in-your-mouth peach cobbler. Mmmm, I get hungry just thinking about it!

Before I left home and discovered fine dining, I indulged in healthy meals like this on a regular basis (Oh, come on, all of the food groups were always there.) Anyway, healthy or not, these dishes are as common to me as a redneck in Texas, but I guess everyone didn't have the same privilege.

"Mmmm, that smells good. What's that?" Peter asked.

Why is it that when minorities are eating anything that hasn't been tossed or chopped, we can never eat in peace at work? After the finger pointing and close breathing, you always seem to lose a smidgen of your hunger.

"Mac and cheese, yams, and oxtails," I answered with my mouth full.

"What's oxtails?" he asked.

I'm at lunch and I'm hungry. I don't have time to teach Soul Food 101.

"Beef."

I don't know why I was bothered. But haven't you noticed that the smallest things set you off during Black History Month? Especially coming to work and being forced to look at *them* the morning after an evening of *Roots*.

"Well, it smells really good."

So, does he want me to offer him some? Maybe next time...

"Thanks."

But some people are bolder...

"Mmm, that smells so good!" Kathy said as she passed by a few minutes later.

"Thanks!"

Keep moving.

"Ooooh, macaroni and cheese. I love macaroni and cheese!"

"Yeah, it's my favorite."

Please don't beg. I have three spoonfuls left, just enough to finish with my oxtails.

"I have to say that it's my specialty," she proclaimed.

Just ask already.

"Yeah, everybody doesn't know how to cook mac and cheese," I said with my mouth full.

"Can I have a bite of yours? I can let you know if it's up to par," she suggested.

Don't you hate it when people justify begging?

"Um, sure."

"Oh, but you just have a few bites left. Are you sure it's okay?"

"Oh, well . . ." I shrugged.

"I just need a tiny bite to see how it compares to mine."

Maybe I missed your show on The Food Network.

"Do you have a fork?" I asked.

Who carries forks with them? Of course she doesn't. Oh, well . . .

"Here, just break it off and put it on this sheet of paper," she insisted.

Damn, I'm trapped!

I felt like a deer caught in the headlights. Call me selfish but I had to wrestle my sturdy fork to break off a "tiny bite." As I watched the small piece move to her lips, I wanted to regain my strength and snatch it back. It's mine! It's mine! But then it disappeared in her greedy mouth.

"Mmmmm, this is really good!"

Yeah, right. I really need your confirmation to know

that I can throw down with mac and cheese. Are you now going to give me another stupid project because I can cook better than you?

"Thanks," I said.

"I must say that this is better than mine. We have to exchange recipes."

Did I ask for your stinky recipe? Why do I want your recipe when mine is better? Just say that you want mine.

Not that I'm not taking full responsibility for good soul food. You can find "real" food in homes of all races, especially in the south. But even though Southerners, black and white, share these menus of down-home cooking, there is still a difference between the two households. One just has more of a kick, if you know what I mean.

"Yeah, we have to do that."

Now can I eat my last two bites of mac and cheese in peace?

"Well, enjoy the rest of your lunch," she said as she finally left me alone to eat in peace.

Thank you!

You would think with all the soul food restaurants that have emerged and have become popular with not just us, but with all races, that *they* wouldn't be surprised every time they see our food. And it never fails, every time they smell it, they have a story to tell about the time they went to this soul food shack in a not-so-nice neighborhood and had the best corn bread on the planet.

"Hey, what's up, girlfriend? You know, your lunch always smell so good," Amy said as she approached me moments after Kathy left my cubicle.

"Thanks."

negro childhood

"What you got today?" she asked.
"Mac and cheese, yams, and oxtails."
"You know what you need?" she suggested.

Maybe peace and quiet so I can enjoy my lunch?

"What?"
"Hot-water corn bread! Have you ever been to Real Soul?"

Just because you want to be down doesn't mean you really are down, homie. How can you even consider a place that sells shrimp fried rice a soul food restaurant?

"Yeah, a couple of times."
"The food is da bomb! Their corn bread is the best I've ever tasted."

That's because you never tasted Aunt Margaret's corn bread.

What makes an expert on soul food? Is it tasting watered-down greens at a subpar restaurant that has the reputation of the best greens in town by a food critic who can't tell the difference between mustards and collards? Or maybe it's dining at a rib shack that claims to have a unique recipe for Texas barbecue sauce that tastes a lot like Kraft? All I know is that I know good soul food like the old woman on the front pew wearing an oversized hat knows every spiritual. I know verse after verse of seasonings and ingredients. I can pick a dish apart, and if I don't know what's missing, I know enough that I can create a better recipe on the spot. But these guests didn't even know the congregational verse. They had never attended a Southern Baptist service. They couldn't feel the music. They hadn't experienced enough hardship to taste the words of the hymn. These people weren't even saved!

Before I took the last scrumptious bite of my macaroni and cheese, I began to think about Auntie's delicious Sunday dinner and how the aroma alone made me smile. Man, that woman knew she could cook!

"Mmmm, that smells good! What we got there?" Miranda asked.

Well, enough of memory lane. I wasn't about to lose my last bite. I immediately shoved my fork in my mouth and interrupted my nostalgic moment. I shook my head with a mouthful of food. "Hmmm-mmm."

i want to be just like you when i grow up

February 18

Dear Diary,

Don't you hate when people try to compare their injustices to the years of confinement, humiliation, separation, confusion, unfairness, discrimination, and unawareness that the black race has endured for all these years? Why do certain groups constantly try to squeeze in our size-ten shoes when they know they have a size-twelve foot? Do they not realize that our ancestors have already broken in our aged shoes with their worn feet? Don't get me wrong, they're still not the most comfortable shoes we own, but because they're basic black we still wear them every day because they seem to go with everything we own.

"We should go to lunch sometime," Matt Stone suggested.

Okay, I'm all for getting to know people.

"I know. When are you free?" I asked.

"What about today?"

"That sounds great. See you at one?"

"I'll come by and pick you up."

So again, I was looking forward to a pleasant lunch with a coworker, Matt from Marketing. I really liked him. He seemed like a nice guy and as hard as it had been, I was really trying to develop friendships at work. We really didn't know each other but he had always been nice when our paths crossed. Always, "hello," "how's it going," "see you later" type of thing. We were around the same age, on the same career level, and little did I know in the same boat, according to him.

He seemed really excited to be in my presence. "It's great that we're finally having lunch."

"Yeah, I'm glad you asked. You know, I'm always too busy to go out."

"I know. They work us like slaves," he admitted.

"But we're just paying our dues, right?"

"Yeah, if that's what they're calling it now."

Oh, I like this guy! Good attitude.

"So how long have you been with the company?" I asked.

"Too long. I know that you've probably noticed, but they're really prejudice."

Prejudice against what—your golf game? I was confused. He was a white male yelling prejudice against a white male-driven company.

I was seriously confused. "What do you mean?"

"Well, you know I'm gay, right?"

negro childhood

"Oh, no, I didn't know."

Really, I had no clue.

"So, see, we're in the same boat."

It's funny how everyone wants to jump in the boat now that it's air-conditioned.

"What do you mean by 'same boat'?" I asked.

"You know, I'm gay, you're black, we all experience the same type of shit."

And lunch was going so well . . .

"The two have nothing to do with each other," I said.

"What? I experience the same prejudices that you do because I'm gay. I can't get certain jobs, and I get the stares. My parents have even disowned me. I know you know what it's like."

For what? For my parents to disown me because I'm black? No, actually I don't have a clue.

I just wanted to have a quiet lunch with a coworker. But that's beginning to look impossible. Should I or shouldn't I? That's the question. Okay, I have no other choice...

"I'm not sure I'm following you. Are you saying that our prejudices are the same?" I asked.

"Are you saying they aren't?" he answered.

Hell, yeah, that's exactly what I'm saying.

"They can't even compare. First of all, I can't hide the fact that I'm black. You can hide your sexuality. I don't have any other choice but to be black. But you can decide tomorrow to pretend to be straight and wave bye-bye to all of the 'prejudice.'"

"Wait, I don't choose to be gay. I am because those were the cards that I was dealt," he explained.

I couldn't believe he thought he was holding the bad hand. We might all be spades, but no matter what order you put them on the table, the ace always beats the king and queen. He could throw out his hand and pick up better cards. Or he could bluff his way through any game. But my hand was filled with the low cards that no one else wanted. There were no more extra cards for me in the stack.

"I don't even think we should go there because you'll never understand or experience the degree of racism that I go through today or my grandfather went through seventy years ago."

"But it's all the same. Prejudice is prejudice. I'm just as much a victim as you are," he insisted.

I said racism, meaning race, not sexual preference.

"You want to talk about a victim? A *black*, gay male, now that's a victim!"

"He's still gay."

"Yeah, and he's also still black."

"Okay, maybe I haven't experienced slavery, but people whisper, and I'm still not accepted everywhere I go," he explained.

Is he serious?

"You know if the only thing black people had to worry about was whispering then we would be in great shape. Don't get me wrong, I'm not saying that gay people have it easy. I know that you have your battles. But they can't even compare to the one that black people have been fighting since slavery."

"Well, I just thought we could relate . . ."

"Maybe on some levels."

Well, I guess he wasn't picking up the check. Damn, I shouldn't have ordered dessert. I can't wait to tell Uncle Sonny about this.

It's funny how when it's convenient, we all want to be the same. I wonder if he would have risked his life so that I could take a sip of water or if he would have gone to jail so I could have a nice view on the bus. I guess you never know. But I did know that we weren't the same. He was comparing apples to oranges. You first have to peel the skin of an orange and then take it apart before you can see its center. But all you have to do is bite into an apple to get to its core. It only takes one bite to even see if it's edible. And if it's too brown, it's considered rotten and tossed in the trash.

He really pissed me off. Why do they feel entitled to freakin' everything we have? They captured our freedom and labor. They stole our creations and talents. They've taken our music and style. And now they want to experience racism too? Can't you give us something that we can call our own? I don't understand. This is just crazy to me!

All of these years, black people have been made to feel that we were not valuable enough for someone to aspire to be like us. But now, everyone, suddenly wants to connect and relate. Boys are trying to dunk basketballs like Vince Carter and spit lyrics like Tupac. Girls are starving to look like Tyra and dance like Janet. "I want to be just like you when I grow up," they say. Black celebrities are hearing that not only from black children, but kids of all races. I hate to be negative and discourage anyone from achieving his goals but there are just some things that aren't possible.

Why do people use us as a role model for injustice? Did his history class not have the one paragraph on black history in America? Was he unaware of the Civil War, the Civil Rights Movement, and even the Holocaust for that matter? It was impossible for Matt to understand and appreciate my people's long, tired journey because his pedicured feet could never endure the troublesome walk of our long, weary past. Come on, I'm not saying that discrimination against homosexuality doesn't exist, but don't freakin' try to compare it to the decades of my struggle. How could he not understand? How could I make him understand? That's the frustrating part because I don't think I can.

i don't wanna hear that funky music

February 23

Dear Diary,

What if we were all the same? Imagine if everyone liked baseball and there was no need for basketball? Or if we all preferred vanilla ice cream and there was no need for the other thirty flavors? What if we all listened to hard rock and there was no need for soul? Would it be so bad? Hell, yeah. It would be torture! It would be mentally impossible to listen to their soulless music note after rhythmless note. I'm not saying that I don't listen to any music besides "black music." And since I've had no other choice and have been exposed to it for the past couple of years, I now have a few rock artists that I enjoy. But for the most part, I need to experience a song like a woman needs to experience love. I need to feel something other than the stiff needle spinning around a hit record.

Peter had become one of my closest coworkers. He hadn't really done anything stupid to piss me off; he was just really cool. After lunch, we always took a break to talk about some of everything. Sometimes we talked about what was on television the night before. Other times the conversation was gossip about other coworkers. But today, the topic was music.

"The Ramones?" he asked.

"Nope," I answered.

"U2?"

"Me too what?"

"The Police?"

"What department?"

"For Christ's sake! Okay, I know you know The Stones."

"Oh, yeah! Mick Jagger!"

"They're legends! Remember 'Brown Sugar'?"

"No, who's that?"

"The Stones! I thought you said you knew their music."

"No, I said I knew Mick Jagger. Didn't Tina Turner teach him how to dance?"

"I can't believe this. Were you sheltered as a kid?"

"No, I listened to a lot of music—Stevie, Marvin, Chaka."

"Yeah, I know them, but I'm talking about real music, you know, rock 'n' roll."

"Where do you think rock 'n' roll came from? Look, for me, music has to have soul. I need to feel the voice and the music."

negro childhood

"Wait, so you're saying that white people don't have soul?"

"No, I'm saying that I prefer R&B because I like soulful music."

"Rock 'n' roll has soul. I can't believe this."

"Look, if I can't move to it, then it doesn't have soul."

"How can you say that? That's just wrong. There have been a lot of great white musicians. The Beatles?"

"Sorry, I prefer The Temptations."

"What? That's just silly."

It's funny, they never had complaints when they forced us to entertain them.

How can he call my preference silly? Had he really listened to "his" original music? Didn't he hear the failed attempts to duplicate our soulful sounds? Their music was as original as a new hip-hop song. How could he tell me what defines good music? We were picking inspirations in the uninspired fields long before they were forced to develop their own music. So now that we're gaining inspiration from our own land, they want to claim that their touristy trips have been more breathtaking than our cultural journeys?

Had he even listened to Marvin Gaye? Had he ever experienced Donny Hathaway? Did he know the contributions of James Brown and Aretha Franklin? And let's not forget our true roots that grew from singers like Mahalia Jackson and James Cleveland. But Peter didn't know nothing 'bout that! He couldn't understand the suffering and joy exerted from their voices. Was he deaf? He couldn't appreciate the lyrics that resulted from mistreatment and misunderstanding. He couldn't feel the music. He couldn't see the history. He couldn't touch the lyrics.

He couldn't smell the medications. He couldn't even hear the voices.

"I have the Beatles's 'Yellow Submarine' in the car. I'm going to go get it so you can hear real music," Peter offered.

I don't wanna hear that funky music.

Isn't it funny how an opinion can turn into fact depending on whose opinion it is? So why is it that his preference overrides mine? How is it that he is going to force me to listen to his music and convince me that my opinions were insignificant and incorrect? But he wasn't looking at it that way. He was the good guy. He was dedicating his time to help a sheltered sista out. He was going to try and teach me all of the things that the poor Negro experience overlooked. He was going to transform me into a Renaissance woman.

As I was listening to the Beatles, I still wasn't impressed.

"See, now this is great music," he said.

"Uh-huh."

"Listen to the instruments, the vocals and the lyrics."

"Uh-huh."

"You can't tell me that these guys weren't amazing."

These guys weren't amazing.

"Uh-huh."

"Wait a minute. Listen to Lennon. Tell me he doesn't know soul."

Him and soul don't even have the same friends.

Had soul become a homonym? Did it mean something totally different than what I had grown to feel? Peter was alone on this one. There was no way he could compare their voices to some of the greats. It seemed that he was the one who needed a lesson on "real" music. Maybe

negro childhood

he needed someone to take an interest in his charitable butt. Had he ever heard the pain in Billie's white gardenia or the blues in Bessie's smooth gin? Had he ever seen the brilliance in Duke's magical wand or the talent in Dizzy's great cheeks? Had he experienced the innovative style of Satchmo and the complex rhythms of Parker? He didn't know nothing 'bout that. While he was trying to convert me into a cultured soul, he was denying himself the enriching experience of great artists, talented writers, and innovative musicians.

Why is it not okay to be different? Why does one have to be right and the other one wrong? Did he know the difference between fact and preference? Had it occurred to him that I, too, was qualified to dictate great music? Had he forgotten that my ancestors had been creating music long before his had claimed rock 'n' roll? I know that carries some weight. I know that our opinions are valid. I know that we know good music. After all of the unforgettable melodies, powerful lyrics and memorable performances, you would think that anyone would find our music entertaining, but I guess when one steals a unique piece of land and strikes oil, there's no need to cultivate it, and there's not even a first thought about splitting the profits with the rightful owner.

let's play, i've got a secret

March 16

Dear Diary,

There are just some things that we shouldn't know. There are other things that we don't care to know. And then there are things that we would never know if people weren't so damn open with their personal lives. Maybe it's just me, but isn't that the purpose of best friends and journals? I'm not saying that my people don't have big mouths. It's just that we tend to tug at other people's skeletons instead of pulling out our own.

    I don't understand why some people are so comfortable with everyone. I don't know your mother; therefore, I don't need to know that she's an alcoholic. I will never meet your sister; therefore, I would have never known that she's a plastic surgery addict. And I didn't even know you had a boyfriend; therefore, I didn't need to know how you satisfy his needs in the bedroom. Aren't parents supposed to teach their children to avoid talking to strangers, especially about personal business? Don't get me wrong, everyone loves to hear a piece of juicy gossip, and I'm included. And everyone gossips every now and then, and I am also included. But usually it's a faux pas for you to be the source of gossip about yourself.

"Good morning," she said.

As she stepped on the elevator, I could tell that something was troubling her. I didn't know her name but I had seen her maybe twice on the elevator before today. I had no interest in how she actually felt but out of habit I asked.

"Hey, how's it going?"

"Horrible. This has been the worst morning of my life."

But you were suppose to say, "fine."

"Oh, I'm sorry."

"Yeah, I'm recovering from an abortion. It's my second. That's why I haven't been at work for the past days," she explained.

I hadn't even noticed. Who are you, again?

"And my stupid, unemployed boyfriend keeps giving me grief but how are we going to bring a child in this world and he hasn't worked for six months because he failed a stupid drug test."

Okay, what do you say to that?

negro childhood

"Oh, I'm sorry," I said.

"Men are worthless. I don't know why I stayed with him after the last affair, but I guess that's love, huh?"

"Yeah, I guess."

"I really need to make another appointment with my therapist. It's so hard, you know?"

Does everyone at this company have a freakin' therapist?

This was worse than playing an all-night game of Monopoly, and I hadn't even been at work ten minutes. I was anxiously waiting for the bright, elevator light moving across the floors to land on mine, so I could have a chance to pass go and get off, but she kept rolling doubles and chances to talk about her wretched personal life.

"So, do you have a boyfriend?"

Again, do I know you?

"Uh, not at the moment."

"Well, you're smart. They're just a waste of your personal space."

Oh, so you do know what the word personal means.

"Well, I wouldn't know because I don't have one."

"But what about in your past?"

I know you don't think that I'm going to discuss my relationships with you. Again, do I know you?

"Yeah, I haven't really had that many."

Can I use my Get Out of Jail Free card?

I was tired of her going around the board in her fancy car, collecting money from passing go and picking up chance cards. It was my turn to roll. But there was nothing on the board that related to me. She had bought all of the railroads, utilities, and blue properties—Park Place and Boardwalk. She was loaded with so much personal crap that I couldn't even compete.

As I moved closer toward the elevator doors, the light finally reached my floor. There I was waiting for the doors to open so I could lose the game of "Let's Talk About Your Personal Life with a Stranger." I stepped off before the elevator came to a complete stop.

"Well, this is my floor. I hope you work everything out."

"You know, I just need to get rid of him," she concluded.

Okay, if that's your decision.

"Well, see you later."

"Yeah, maybe we can do lunch?" she suggested.

But I don't want to play anymore!

"Uh, sure. That would be great."

Yeah! The bank had finally run out of money! The doors began to close when she pulled them open again. Had she found a blue fifty?

"I feel so stupid for asking you this . . ."

Well, you didn't feel stupid when you were telling me about your secret abortion and cheating druggie.

"What?"

"What's your name again?"

Well, I guess I made some ground. They're starting to share everything. Actually, probably more than they need to with me. But the point is that they're comfortable with me. And it seems that I'm also getting comfortable with myself being around them as well. I knew that this could work; everything takes time. It feels like they're really looking past the color thing and just accepting me as their own. I hate to brag, but I said it would happen, and it looks like I was right.

1. ~~See Opportunity~~
2. ~~Taste Acceptance~~
3. Hear Comfort
4. Touch Life
5. Breathe Success

negro childhood

March 18

Dear Diary,

Who doesn't love children? It's just something about their innocence and potential that draws you to them and forces a smile. For this reason, I guess you can say that the people at work are beginning to recognize my growth of what they perceive as my childhood. They have begun to give me positive affirmations to build my esteem. My special talents amuse them because they are reminded of the freedom associated with being a kid. It seems that

I can't do any wrong—I am somehow the spoiled kid on the block. I'm not sure if they are trying to make up for my nigger birth or just trying to develop a child who they could be proud to call their own. Either way, I guess I will enjoy it while it lasts.

But sometimes grownups can still be a little overbearing. Ever since they had acknowledged that I was smart enough to start learning the ABC's of their workplace, they are constantly around to make sure I am developing properly so they can take credit for my special achievements. Their expectations are gradually becoming higher because I am walking on my own. They are determined to make me everything that they had always dreamt of becoming. So, their vision has become my sight. They are living through their Negro child.

Yeah, you heard me correctly. Times are changing and so are the perceptions in my workplace. I am no longer the uneducated slave who was brought in to work for them. I have proven to them that I can work and think without being forced to work and think. Therefore, they have decided to free me from treating me like a baby who they could rock to their side. Instead, they are starting to recognize me as the child who they think can be molded into a carbon copy of them.

I admit, I wasn't quite aware of my environment when I first arrived. And I also admit that I have grown over the past months, accepting my new way of life. But thanks to the teachings of Mama and them, I never really acted immature about any of my inexperienced situations. However, my coworkers still insist on make-believing the stereotypical traditions, so to them my imaginary friend still walks on my heels. But it just seems they are now starting to accept my loyal companion.

colored adolescence

March 25

Dear Diary,

I hated being a teenager. I guess you can say adolescence was a critical time in my life. I began to use everything that I had learned and memorized from my childhood to create my uniqueness. Yet, I was limited to where and how I could express it. What's a girl to do? I had no other choice but to find ways around the conventional system. I had to sneak my own style into my self-expression. I was forced to go against a majority that I wasn't feelin'. I had to make choices for myself and not for others' approval. I guess that's all a part of growing up.

I was also accustomed to living without any real responsibilities and set rules. It was around this time in my life, that all of the unforeseen boundaries began to hover over my freedom. So you can understand my reason for rebelling against certain restrictions. Of course there were rules that I accepted. And I still knew my place in the different classes of society. I was ordered not to walk into certain settings that could offer me a broader view of living. I was told what to say, what not to say, when to say it and when not to say it. I was banned from prosperous places because of my possible influence. But I suddenly outgrew certain games and hobbies and slowly began searching for something that would not only occupy my time, but could fulfill my bottomless bowl of potential. I was also beginning to experience my firsts: first kiss, first job, first car. However, it seemed like everything I embraced was criticized and disregarded by those who thought they knew better because they had lived a little bit longer.

For some reason as teenagers, we are always forced to live and see the world through experienced eyes; however, those same conservative eyes are never forced to enter what they perceive as our trivial world. This was something that I wasn't used to since I had lived freely during my childhood years. I was encouraged to imagine. And as a teenager that was somehow taken away.

no shoes, no service

April 4

Dear Diary,

"Never put yourself in uncomfortable positions." That's what Aunt Margaret used to say.

"If you can't be comfortable in your own home, then you can't be comfortable nowhere."

That one belonged to Aunt Billie.

After sitting in my bare cubicle for six months, I began to understand the logic behind their beliefs. My feet were tired of being in heels all day. They wanted to be free, to stretch out on the table, to relax; they wanted to be comfortable! And I was finally ready to oblige. I knew I still couldn't walk around the office barefoot but I felt that I wouldn't accidentally step in anything in my small, spotless space, so, I decided it was time to get comfortable in my little studio—to decorate my cubicle.

I wanted to put up things that inspired me. You know, just add little touches of comfort so it would appear that someone lived there instead of the vacant look that it had occupied for months. I also knew that I couldn't go overboard because the homeowner association still had to approve all changes. That meant nothing that couldn't blend in with the rest of the office's décor. And of course as soon as I put the pushpin in the last picture that I was hanging up, Lisa found her way over to my cubicle.

"Oh, so you decorated your cubicle. Who's that?" she asked.

"Maya Angelou."

"Oh, that's the poet woman."

"Yeah."

"Oh, are you related to her?" she asked.

"No."

"Then why do you have a picture of her hanging up?"

"Why do you have a picture of Madonna in your cubicle?" I asked.

"Because I love her. She's amazing!"

"Then I love Maya."

Why go there? Even if I explained my reasons to Lisa, she wouldn't understand. She would wonder, *Why is she still living in the past? Slavery is over. It's not like my father ever owned slaves.*

Later in the day, another tourist visited my new attractive space.

"Hey! So you finally decided to decorate your cubicle," Miranda said, surprisingly.

The only reason she decided to stop by was because Lisa probably told her nosy butt.

"Yeah, I was tired of sitting in an empty space."

"What's that?" she asked.

colored adolescence

When I turned around and looked at the target of Miranda's pointed finger, I saw the *Essence* magazine that I received in the mail the night before.

"Oh, that's this month's *Essence*. I haven't had a chance to read it."

Not that I was afraid she was going to ask to borrow it and not give it back.

She picked it up and began to thumb through it.

"What's *Essence*?" she asked.

"It's like a black version of *Marie Claire* or *Cosmo*."

"Oh, Angela Basett! Isn't she beautiful? You know, you kinda look like her."

Of course, we all look alike. Even though, Angela and I look like we couldn't even be in-laws.

"Why do you have to have a black version of *Cosmo*?" she asked. "I mean, don't you think that's what's wrong now? We're always trying to be separate."

No, she did not just go there! Please tell me she did not go there.

At that moment, I had no choice. She was on my territory and declaring war. This was a battle that I had no choice but to fight.

"Well, that would be fine if those magazines profiled black actresses besides the Halles or featured pieces on black hair and makeup. But they don't."

"Halle's beautiful. You don't like Halle Berry?" she asked, shocked.

Did I say I didn't like Halle?

"No, I didn't say that. I'm just saying that the only black actresses you see in the mainstream magazines are those who are known and accepted by white America."

"I've seen black celebrities who I didn't know in *Cosmo*," she claimed.

"Not in a feature article."

"But don't you think you're separating yourself when you get your own magazine?"

"I haven't separated myself; America has by not considering my consumer needs," I explained.

"See, it always goes back to let's blame America. Why can't we forget slavery? Yes, it was wrong but we can't harp on the past forever."

"That's easy for you to say because you're not really affected by the past. But even if I try to forget it, America always reminds me."

"What do you mean?" she ignorantly asked.

"I mean, I get service depending upon which boutique I walk into. But you're guaranteed it every time. I have to prove my intelligence by showing not only a degree but by speaking to expose my vocabulary, but you can be silent and still be perceived as an educated woman."

"That's not true. Look at you, you're not like normal black people," she said.

Okay, I had to get a little attitude, but can you really blame me? "What do you mean by normal?"

"You know, you have a degree and you don't talk black."

"How many black people do you know?" I asked.

"Well, you," she admitted.

"So, if I'm the only one you know, how are you going to judge an entire race by what you see on TV? If that were the case, I would think that you were a rich white girl with no self-esteem looking to fit in wherever you can."

"What do you mean by that?"

I knew that one was going to fly right over her head.

colored adolescence

She continued, "Anyway, by not merging together, you're keeping the stereotypes going."

"You know what? This isn't about me. It's about the media, giving just enough to avoid complaints. If everything is so good, then do you think there would be a need for *Essence* and BET? If we should all read one magazine, then why don't you buy *Essence*? You know what? If we should all watch one show, then why don't you watch *Living Single* instead of *Friends*? Oh, I forgot, *Living Single* isn't on the air anymore."

"What's *Living Single*?"

"My point exactly," I answered.

"Well, I still don't get it."

"And you probably never will."

"What is it, a black thang?" she asked sarcastically.

No, she didn't!

"No, it's an American thang," I said.

What the hell? I can't wait to tell Mama about this. Was it too soon? Okay, so now I know. It wasn't time for me to completely relax. I had to work a little harder and prove that I, too, deserved spa days. I still had to massage my presence into their small minds. I had to scrub a little bit harder to exfoliate the living stereotypes that remained on their dead ancestors' skin. I needed to find a formula to rejuvenate their souls to accept change and progress for what it is, a positive thing and not a separation plot. But I also needed to remember that I could never walk around barefoot; I still had to slide on my flimsy slippers while lingering through their first-class resort.

Maybe I should have waited a couple more weeks before I took off my shoes. I mean, I hadn't even left my space and still I was bitten by something. My feet were blistering, but my temper was scorched. Who in the hell did she think she was coming into my space lecturing me about world unity? How was she qualified to educate me on right and wrong when the only thing that she had said right was "hey?" But you know I had to stay cool. I couldn't fight her ignorance with my anger. But I still had to put her in check. And after I was done, her stupidity was still defeated by my calmness. And they wonder why we can't stand them sometimes!

melt in your mouth, not in your hands

April 27

Dear Diary,

We all have our weaknesses. And no matter how hard we try to justify them to others, they just never seem to have the same effect for anyone else. And even though we know the consequences of judgment, we still have the need to experience that captivating feeling of capturing our weak point one more time. I'm sure you understand what I'm saying. Like I said, we all have at least one weakness. For me, it's Luther Vandross's songs. For my mama, it's red tulips. For my best friend, it's strawberries and cream. For the women in my office, it's chocolate.

Lately, there has been a small group of people who I've decided had friendship potential so I have been hanging out with them after work. All of my close friends are back home in Texas and it has been really hard to meet other black folks like me. Since I moved here from college, I have been surrounded by nothing but white people. But come on, they're not all bad. Actually, I've been feeling like I'm just one of the guys with them instead of the black girl. Who knew?

The spot was this bar across the street from the office because it seems that they are all obsessed with bars for some reason, which is cool because I have grown accustomed to the pastime of hanging out in a smoke-filled local bar. Of course, there's usually not that many black folks guzzling down drinks. But that's also cool because I've gotten used to that too.

For some reason Amy was excited about something. "So, I met this guy at the grocery store last night. I told him to stop by tonight."

"How does he look?" I asked.

"Well, he's tall and built. And he has the most gorgeous skin!"

"What do you mean?" Diane asked.

"It's so smooth and clear. Oh, look! There he is!"

As I turned to look toward the door, I did a double take. Now, I'm fine with interracial dating. I really am. I just don't like to see a fine brotha with a skinny white chick. But other than that, I'm all for dating outside my race. And yes, he was a brotha. And yes, he was fine. And yes, Amy is a skinny white chick.

"Eric! Over here!" Amy yelled.

Why is it that they have to satisfy their sweet tooth with smooth, rich dark chocolate? I mean isn't there other hard candy that will do the job? Is it a plot to get back at their men for forcing chocolate desserts down their mouths in the past and gaining the weight of offspring? Or are they tired of watching their straight figures and now trying to develop curves. Or maybe now that there are more gourmet chocolates on the market, they finally think it's worth indulging in their secret fantasy.

"Hey! Good to see you again."

As she introduced him to everyone around the table, he kept glancing my way. What? Was he waiting for my approval? Or was he gloating over his capture of another one? What was his reason? I know there had to be an ulterior motive. Why else would he choose a cousin over a sista? Now, I can understand why a black woman would try a lower calorie treat; a quality piece of chocolate was becoming a rare treat these days. But what reason would a strong black man have for not choosing to honor his sturdy figure with the ultimate, satisfying chocolate dessert. I mean, who likes a scrawny man?

Amy was anxious to get reacquainted with Eric. "Let's go get a drink at the bar?"

"Okay, it was nice to meet you guys."

Another one . . . gone.

As soon as the two stepped far enough from the table, Paige and Diane started to go back and forth with their score on the quality of chocolate Amy had found.

"Oh, he's seems nice," Paige started.

"Yeah, I would love to taste him," Diane confessed.

"Did you guys see his skin? It's so smooth," Paige said.

"I wish I could touch it," Diane said.

"Racey, how come black people have such great skin?" Paige asked.

Oh, please don't start with the stupid questions.

" I don't know," I answered.

"I bet he's great in bed. Oh, I just love a strong, dark man," Diane said.

Didn't they know that gluttony was one of the seven deadly sins? But I guess it didn't matter. For years, their pride and greed have been the reason for their sloth and anger toward those who they have lusted and envied.

But really, I started to think, did I have the right to get upset at his right to choose? It's not like we've always had this freedom. He can whistle at any woman he wanted. He no longer had to pass unrelated tests to prove that he could read the menus at dinner or prove that his grandfather had dated her grandmother. In order to exercise his preference, he just made a choice. And it was his right. And if he was just voting for what was right for him then how could I be mad? I mean our ancestors fought for equality and to be seen not by the color of their skin but by the content of their character. So, how could I have a problem with her seeing him as just a man and him seeing her as just a woman?

I'm still not sure that I'm feeling it one hundred percent, but hey, what can you do?

"Hey, beautiful!"

As I turned around to respond to the lame pickup line, I was suddenly speechless. There he was, standing behind me with a manly drink in his hand to complement his manly body. Everything was perfect but there was one problem. He wasn't a brotha. I know. I know. There's nothing wrong with being a cousin. I mean, I've been one for a while back at the office. And I had just come to terms with our brothas preferring white chocolate a few minutes ago. But there's one small problem: I don't like white chocolate! I'm used to the rich and smooth taste of semi-sweet chocolate or the deep flavor of dark chocolate

colored adolescence

straight from the grinding mill. I've even had a little milk in my chocolate with a mellow flavor.

But I've never craved the sweet, milky taste of white chocolate. Is it even considered real since there are no chocolate solids mixed in? I was a little impressed that this piece of imitation chocolate would even want to blend with a scoop of cocoa. I know that I wasn't as dark as most types but I was still strong in flavor.

This was the first piece in a long time that had even tempted me into wanting to take a bite. For the past couple of months, I had been on a diet because I was trying to lose the weight that my last piece of chocolate had left me. So, why shouldn't I experiment? White chocolate has become acceptable over the years. Just because the family recipe required melted dark chocolate didn't mean white chocolate wouldn't dissolve if that's the only thing the grocery store had in stock, right? I know that it wouldn't taste the same but it still could satisfy my sweet tooth.

So, what the hell, right?

"Well, hello," I answered.

to be young, gifted, and black professional

May 19

I was looking good! As soon as I stepped off the elevator, I felt the envious, starstruck stares. There I was in my stylish, classy heels that slimmed my legs; fitted, but conservative skirt that accentuated my curves; a bohemian blouse that not only made my two soldiers stand at attention but proved I had my own style; hip, unique accessories that flattered my round face, as well as my total look; and of course my fresh mini-braids that were gathered in a vibrant scarf that complemented my silk, caramel skin: I was the poster child for "black professional."

The eyes followed every secure step I made across the room to my cubicle. And, of course, when I landed, a bunch of fans started to circle, not only to ask for my autograph, but they all wanted to know how I became a superstar and advice on how they, too, could become famous.

I kept getting various questions and touches all day. "Wow! Your hair looks fabulous!"

"How did you do that?"

"How did you grow your hair that fast?"

"Did it hurt?"

I felt like a newborn that everyone wanted a chance to hold. I didn't mind. I kinda enjoyed the attention. But instead of just taking their turn to touch the hair and say, "That's nice," some of course had to tickle and pry until I became agitated.

Of course, the first comment was from nosy Lisa.

"You look just like that singer, uh, Brandy. How did they do that?" Lisa asked.

"It's just braided into my hair," I answered.

"Oh! At first I thought that maybe you had a secret on how to grow hair."

"No, my real hair is still the same length," I explained.

"What do you mean real hair? So, this isn't your hair?"

It's funny, they know every lyric to our music and all the dance steps from our videos, but whenever it involves something they can't learn or enjoy, they're ignorant. But to be fair, I guess, why would they know? I don't know the number for the "perfect" shade of blond. However, I don't become bitter or envious when I'm not invited to the blond convention. And I'm not totally ignorant to the maintenance of white hair. So, why can't they have just a little knowledge of mine? I know it's not important, but hell, we all had to learn algebra.

"It's so pretty! Can I touch it?"

"Sure."

As Paige ran her fingers through my hair, she professed, "Ooh, it feels so soft and silky, so real."

"It is real."

"How is it real?"

"It's human hair," I explained.

"How do they do that?"

"I don't know. It comes in a package."

"Do you think I could sell some of my hair and have it packaged?" she wondered.

"I don't know."

"How much do you think I can get for my hair? It's just as long as this. Actually, mine may even be silker."

"I don't know," I said again.

And don't you just hate when you have to explain the process, like you have a cosmetologist license? Later in the morning, Diane asked her round of questions.

"You look gorgeous! How long did that take?" Diane asked.

"Sixteen hours."

"When did you sleep?"

"It wasn't a straight sixteen hours. We took breaks."

"But did you have to sit still?" she asked.

"Yeah, while she was braiding."

"And how did she do it exactly?"

"It's just like when you braid your hair," I explained. "And then she just braided the human hair into mine. Afterward, she glued the ends so it doesn't come apart."

"Oh, that isn't all your hair?"

See what I mean. It was explanation after explanation. I think I told the story more than a child hears the word *no*. But school was far from over. Weaves 202 was too advanced for some people so I eventually had to teach Black Hair 101.

"That's amazing! But, can you shampoo it everyday?" Miranda asked.

"Why would I wash it every day?"

I knew where this was going, but I decided to play along.

"Don't you shampoo your own hair every day?" she asked.

"No."

"What? How do you not wash your hair every day?" she asked, disgusted.

"Black women don't have to wash our hair everyday because our hair isn't as oily as white hair."

She was somewhat disgusted. "Arrgh! That's gross. Doesn't it smell?"

"No."

"Doesn't it get dirty?"

"See, you have oily hair. So, when you wash your hair every day, you still have oil," I started to explain, "but I don't. So, if I washed my hair every day, it would strip the little oil that I do have. And it's no big deal because our hair is used to not being shampooed everyday."

Suddenly she had discovered a conventional method that she, too, could possibly try. "Well, maybe I should stop shampooing my hair every day. It's been really dry lately."

"I don't know."

Will that school bell ring? I'm so tired of teaching the slow children.

My mama used to say, "be careful what you wish for," and she is so right. I was soon faced with the valedictorian of black knowledge, Amy.

"It's so beautiful! So, how long does that last?"

"About three months," I answered for the tenth time.

"Wow! That's great that you don't have to do anything for three months. I remember when I tried to do that to my hair. It didn't even last two days. The braids wouldn't stay. Probably because your hair is thicker than mine."

"Maybe," I said, shrugging.

"So, what do you do when you sleep?"

Oh, a question for me? I thought you knew.

"I just sleep with a scarf."

"Maybe I can try it again. Do you think it will work this time?"

"What?"

"You know, braiding my hair," she said.

Do you tell her what she wants to hear or what she needs to hear?

"Umm."

"Well, you know, Bo Derek started it all," she exclaimed.

You have to know when to pick your battles, and this is one where I just can't walk away.

"Excuse me?" I asked.

"Didn't you see the movie *Ten*?"

"Yeah, but who do you think Bo Derek stole it from?"

"If I'm not mistaken, she started it," she insisted.

"Actually, she didn't. Braiding was around decades before Bo Derek. It originated in Africa."

"Are you sure?"

"Positive."

"Oh. Well, I have to get back to work."

Some people just don't want to learn. What can you do? It was funny because after that discussion, no one approached me for the rest of the day to compliment my new hairdo. I'm sure that Amy had told the entire floor about my resistance to accept that their ancestors had created "everything." That was probably why Kathy got involved.

"Can I talk to you for a moment?" Kathy asked.

"Sure."

"It's about, how can I put this? I'm not sure if you're dressed appropriately for our work environment."

"What do you mean? I wasn't aware that there was

a strict dress code on Fridays. You're in jeans and a T-shirt."

"Well, yeah, but I was actually talking about your head wrap. I think that it falls under the no baseball caps rule."

"But it's not a cap."

"Yeah, that's where there's a gray line because what would you call it?"

"Culture."

"Oh, is it a black—I mean African-American—tradition?"

"No, it isn't. And it's not a baseball cap either."

She decided to back down because the last thing she wanted on a Friday afternoon was a confrontation, especially with a black—I mean African-American—woman.

"I'm sorry if I offended you. It's just that I wasn't sure."

"No, no problem. I'm glad I could be of some help. Now you know that it's not a baseball cap."

"Oh, okay. Well, I have to get going. I just want you to know that you're doing a fantastic job and you're an asset to this company."

She had watched one too many management tapes, but if that's what it took to end this stupid conversation, so be it.

"Thank you."

"And you look so nice today. I love your hair," she added.

"Thanks."

I'm gonna wear another head wrap on Monday just to piss her off.

the ebonics syndrome

May 28

Dear Diary,

Everybody wants to be a hero. Everyone tries to make a difference. Everybody wishes to affect a life. Everyone has a desire to be a part of a miracle. But not everyone is born to practice medicine. Why do they always look at us as a patient instead of a colleague? Why do they constantly try to administer vaccinations to prevent outbreaks of our culture? Are they so cautious because they think that it's contagious? Do they not realize that they are immune from certain aspects of our culture? They are so stupid. I really don't mean to group the entire white race together in one big bottle, but I'm pissed! I'm not saying that I agree with stereotyping any one group of people, but after today, I understand how one could make that mistake.

"I'm just going to axe Kathy when she gets back," I replied.

"What did you say?" Peter asked.

"When?"

"Just now. What did you say you were going to do?"

"What do you mean?" I asked.

"You said you were going to do something to Kathy."

"What? I said I was going to talk to her when she gets back."

"No, no. You said something else," Peter insisted.

"No, I didn't."

"Yeah, you did. You were going to . . ."

"What are you talking about?" I questioned.

"You said that you were going to *axe* Kathy when she gets back."

"Oh yeah, that's what I said. So, what's wrong? You don't want me to talk to her about it?"

"It's not *axe*. It's *ask*," he explained.

You've got to be fuckin' kidding me!

"What?" I snapped.

"It's ask."

"I know that it's ask. What's your point?"

"It's just that *axe* is not proper English."

Segregation wasn't "proper," but you guys screamed that for years.

"Excuse me, Peter. I wasn't aware that I was being tested on my English."

"No, I didn't mean to make you uncomfortable. I was just trying to help."

"Help with what?" I asked.

"I'm not like most people. I understand that just

colored adolescence

because you use incorrect English doesn't mean you're stupid. But other people may see it as a drawback."

I know he didn't! Okay, I can't let this one fall off my shoulder.

"What do you mean by drawback?"

"Look, ebonics or whatever you want to call it just feed into the stereotypes of black people, but for some reason you guys persist on using it. And you wonder why you are perceived as less than someone who can actually hold an intelligent conversation."

What the hell?

"Maybe we persist because suddenly 'you guys' have popularized using ebonics, slang, or whatever you think is the correct word. And what you're saying is ridiculous. If you say 'hey' or 'what's up' instead of 'hello,' even though you're familiar with hello and its meaning, does that make you stupid?"

You're the dumb ass.

"No, that's not what I'm saying. I'm saying that . . ."

Just shut up! You don't even know what you're saying right now.

"Oh, I got one even better," I interrupted. "If you have a southern accent and say 'y'all' instead of 'you guys' does that make you dumb?"

"No, it's different. A regional accent is a part of a person."

"Oh, so I guess ebonics isn't," I said.

"No, I guess it is in a way, but it's still incorrect English."

"But I'm not saying it's correct. I know it isn't, but I use it because it's just as much a part of me just as a southern accent is a part of someone in the south. And I know when and when not to use it. Like if I were in a big meeting, I would say *ask*. But if I'm in a casual environment, sure, I might say *axe*. If anything, I would say that that's intelligence because I know when and when not to use it."

And I know you're just stupid.

"Look, I don't want to get into an argument about it. I was just trying to help."

Help whom exactly? Do we try to cure their disease of shortening everyone's name—Jen (Jennifer), Melis (Melissa), Ame (Amy), or Ang (Angie)? Why do they do that?

Why is "help" their excuse for every situation once there's mayhem? They're always claiming to save our lives while poisoning us with their prescriptions at the same time. Haven't they learned that we're immune to their drugs? Their experiments of high levels of shouts and threats didn't influence the determination of the nine young patients in Little Rock. Their explosive procedure of the four innocent patients in Birmingham didn't stop the fight for a healthy life. You would think that they would have come up with a different antidote by now. But like I said earlier, everyone just doesn't have what it takes to operate on our strong will and brilliant minds.

And the next time you step to me trippin' like that, I'm gonna gat yo' ass, fo' real though!

just a group of us
June 3

Dear Diary,

Fear. Everyone's afraid of something.

1. Spiders
2. Planes
3. Dying
4. Thrillers
5. Snakes
6. Change
7. Pain
8. Dark

Oh, I almost forgot . . . three or more black co-workers standing around laughing and talking about nothing that has to do with nothing in a corner. Why are people so afraid of us? You just expect that a bag will be gripped tighter when you walk next to someone on the street but not in the workplace. It's supposed to be different, right? No assumptions. No stereotypes, but I guess my office didn't get that memo.

There had been a recent push to diversify the company and employ more African-Americans in career-type positions. Two minorities had been added to the all-white diversity council and together they brilliantly came up with affirmative action. Afterward, Adam Levy, the president of the company, called a big meeting where he announced that the company was creating three new positions where minorities would be given an opportunity to gain exposure and experience. And of course that created an immediate feeling of animosity toward the minorities brought in to fill these positions, which some people in the office felt were rightfully theirs or a family friend's who they wanted to get into the company.

But it wasn't like they thought of the brilliant idea to expand the family on their own. Actually, a lawsuit from two employees downstairs was the mastermind behind the plan. But of course, they would never give credit where it was due and admit their real motive because then it would look as if they were sweeping the problem under the rug. And we all know they don't do brooms; that's a job for the people downstairs.

It felt good to finally feel alone with somebody else. So, as you can guess, I immediately bonded with the three new people of the small office. Derek Roberts was a recent college graduate who was still overqualified to work as a new accounts trainee. Craig Washington had a master's that intimidated the hell out of Kathy so she kept a close eye on her new, educated assistant. Nicole Adams was in

colored adolescence

her last year of school and was hired as the office intern for the semester. They were all cool people. We always found time to shoot the breeze but sometimes we had to strategize to do it.

"Hey, what y'all talking about?" Derek asked as he approached Craig and me in a vacant corner.

Uh-oh, there are now three...

So, of course, people started to take notice of the situation, especially Peter, the ebonics debater who stood across the way. Three black coworkers talking and laughing. *Are they talking about me? Are they discussing the inappropriate comment that was made the other day? Are they laughing at me?*

"Nothing. We were just talking about a comedy showcase I went to last night," I explained.

"Was it any good?" Derek asked.

"Yeah, they had some pretty funny comics."

"Where was it?"

"Oh, at this new spot on Pico. It was really nice."

And then Nicole joined the group. "Hey, guys, what's going on?"

Uh-oh, and then there were four...

I guess Peter felt like he had to put a stop to the conspiracy forming so...

"Oh, Nicole, can you find the projections file for me?"

"Sure."

We picked up where we left off...

"Nothing. Can't wait 'til Friday gets here," Craig answered.

"What are y'all doing this weekend?" Derek asked.

"I think I'm going to just chill and watch the playoffs. Hey, maybe I'll cook and have some people over," I suggested.

"I'm in," Derek said.

"Yeah, me too," Craig added.

"What do you want me to bring?" Nicole asked.

As Kathy passed the group on her way to the rest room, which was weird considering she had just passed us coming back from the rest room a minute ago, she began to wonder. Four black coworkers planning an event. Were they forming a religion to separate themselves and gain independence? But then they would refuse to worship us. Was this new plot because of the inappropriate comment I made to Craig last week? I didn't realize he had caught that. What was this new religion? Who was their honorable leader?

"No, I got it. Y'all don't have to bring anything," I insisted.

"Are you sure 'cause we've tasted your famous chocolate cake?" Craig recalled.

"No, no, I told y'all. I just kept it in the oven too long that time."

"Yeah, sure!" Nicole said laughing.

Once again, there was laughter within the group. And once again, there was the fear that we were planning "something" throughout the office. Were we conspiring to create waves in the now calm sea? Were we gloating over the two employees' victory?

"Oh, I forgot to tell you guys what Lisa did yesterday," Derek began.

"What did she do this time? I can't stand her," Craig said.

As he started to whisper, Kathy walked by for the fourth time. *Why are they whispering? Are they planning another lawsuit? Are they unhappy? Because the last thing we want to do is to make them unhappy, considering the consequences of the last two unhappy black employees. What do they want now, the office is only on five acres?*

colored adolescence

"Oooh, I can't believe she did that," I said.

"Okay, good I was just thinking it was me," Derek said.

"No, she know she was wrong," Nicole assured.

"I know, but I didn't know if I was overreacting," Derek said.

"Naw, she's just stupid like that," I offered.

"Yeah, I wouldn't even waste the energy thinking about it," Nicole advised.

And Peter was back . . .

"Oh, sorry to interrupt again, guys, but Nicole, I really need that file."

"No problem. See y'all later."

As she left, she gave us the same look that we were giving her. Peter knew good and well he didn't need that funky file. Come to think of it, I had never seen him "need" a file before today. What he needed was to calm his nerves and assure himself that he hadn't done anything wrong the other day.

"Well, we should get back to work," I said.

"Yeah, they're probably having a fit. There's more than two of us talking," Craig said.

"Conspiracy!" we all yelled.

"See you later. And let me know if you change your mind about us bringing something," Derek said as he walked away.

"Okay, talk to you later."

And then there was one...

It just feels good to relax, even if it's just for five minutes, and even if it makes them a little nervous. It's funny because there are cliques all over the office. But the four of us aren't a part of any of them and didn't feel the need to try and sneak our way into one. We didn't need anyone to validate our self-worth. But that's why they were afraid. We are all strong minded with our own individual personality. There was no defined leader and set attitudes. So the four of us combined equaled the power of four leaders instead of one. And that made them think of the effect Martin, Malcolm, Medgar, and Mandela would have marching together in the same protest, and that could wreak havoc.

But, it was okay if they rallied together because there's no *I* in team. They gossiped in peace and they laughed without suspect. But as soon as our group decided to meet to shoot the breeze, they were ready to try and hose our gatherings down with subtle stares and obvious distractions. And they wonder why we don't understand them sometimes.

did i say that?

June 30

Dear Diary,

We all make mistakes. And for some of us, there are even consequences. Sometimes it costs us an arm and a leg. And other times we pay with our heart. There have also been incidents where mistakes have cost us our freedom and others when we've paid with our life. I'm all for forgiving and granting people a second chance to correct a wrongdoing but sometimes there are things you can't take back and things you can't ignore. There are some things you just can't forget.

1. Cheating
2. Lying
3. Stealing
4. Killing

5. Dirty kids at church
6. Men in pink (never looks good)
7. Bad breath
8. Ignorance

No matter how many times you try to free them, there are those present mistakes that continue to suspend from your mind just as the ripe fruit dangled from the trees of the past.

"So, how's your house hunting going?" I asked Paige as she passed by my cubicle.

"I'm still looking. I didn't realize how hard it would be to find a place."

"Don't worry, you'll find your dream home," I assured her.

See, I've been developing relationships with people at work. I'm not always the angry black worker. I didn't feel different when I hung out with some and she was still one of them. With her, I rarely felt the black and white thing. See, I knew that they couldn't be all bad.

I had been helping Paige house hunt on weekends, and she had come close so many times. But I guess that's what we had in common. We were both strong women who refuse to settle on anything that was important for us.

"So, I thought you were going today to look at something."

"I did, but you should have seen the neighbors. Frank and I would never live next door to ghetto people," she said.

colored adolescence

What she meant to say was, "we would never live next door to black people, we just work with them…"

I actually believe that sometimes my coworkers forget that just because I don't exemplify the false stereotypes of black people, that I am still black. And when they belittle my people, they belittle me.

And we're suppose to be the unintelligent race.

"What do you mean ghetto?" I asked. "I thought you looked in Forest Pine. That's a nice neighborhood."

"It is but there's this young African-American family next door. They have to be drug dealers to afford a house like that. You know, you just know these things by looking at some people."

And she still doesn't realize that she's talking to a black person. I know that I'm not as dark as Uncle Sonny, but damn.

"What do you mean?" I asked again.

"You know. Nice cars, nice house. How else could they afford that?"

Well I wouldn't know since according to you, I'm exempt from that lifestyle.

"Maybe they have good jobs. You know, we're not all drug dealers," I said jokingly.

Ding, ding, ding! The bell finally went off.

"Oh, I wasn't . . . I mean, I didn't mean it like that. You know I consider you a friend," she said, finally finding the right words.

Oh, so could my cousin be your friend? Or am I the only one because I don't have my family's nose?

"Yeah, I know."

I tried. Lord knows I tried to look past the race thing. I tried to ignore our differences and concentrate on our similarities. I thought it was going well. How could she betray my trust of her intelligence? And they wonder why we are so leery . . .

On a good note, at least now I know where Paige stands on mistaken identity since she thinks "we all look alike." Maybe it's a trait that's inherited. Maybe it was her great-grandmother who mistakenly identified my great-grandfather as the "nigger" who raped her. Or maybe it was her great-uncle who lynched my great-aunt because he thought she was the "negro" who stole his money, which he later discovered he misplaced. You would think that we learn from our mistakes. But for some people, they are just unknown habits that are handed down like family heirlooms.

Mistakes. We all make them. We all want to be forgiven for them. But how can we ask for forgiveness when we don't even know we're committing an error? Paige didn't even realize that she had said something not only wrong, but inappropriate. She wasn't aware that she had degraded me to my face. She had no clue that she had condemned a family for life because their shade resembled the guy she had seen on the nightly news.

How can you forget something like that? What can you do? I knew that I couldn't carry the anger on my shoulders. But you can't ignore "true" feelings. You can't disregard their disregard. You can't forget the ignorant mistakes. And I couldn't avoid them. I had to face them every day and I couldn't face them with hurt and anger. I was bigger than that. I had to chalk it up and move on to the next day. But even though I had no choice but to erase the visible betrayal, I still had to remember the formula that was written on the board of truth. Because I'm sure I would get tested on it again later.

Sure, they have revised and added to the mistakes of

colored adolescence

the past to make them less noticeable but the meaning is still there. They're just stuck in your mind like the words to the Pledge of Allegiance. They're glued to your heart the same as your rested right hand as you stand to recite it. But how can "every" person bestow loyalty to a society that promises a freedom that entitles them to pursue life, liberty and happiness when mistakes prevent them from experiencing just and fair treatment?

baby, I'm a star!

July 17

Dear Diary,

1. I'm so stupid!
2. I look fat in this!
3. I'm so ugly!
4. I look disgusting!
5. I am such a pig!
6. I need more sun. I look like a ghost!
7. Maybe plastic surgery will fix my nose!
8. Who's going to marry me with this body?
9. I'm such a retard!

We all have our days where we just don't feel our best. You know the ones where you just feel icky and unattractive and no matter what you put on or take off, you still see atrocious? Or the days that we can't seem to meet anything right and keep bumping into everything wrong. Yeah, we've all had at least one of those. But as usual, our reactions are always different from theirs. On days when we're not the brightest star in the sky, we still never give up our opportunity to shine. We just give off the little light we can, even if it's just a dim sparkle. But not the women in my office. They will put themselves down until they eventually become a falling star.

"I'm so stupid! I'm so sorry, I forgot to fax that letter," Kelly Gruber apologized. "Hopefully, it's not too late."

Not that I disagree, but don't knock yourself out like that.

Today was Kelly's, Brenden's niece, first day. She had been given the job that Nicole was promised a week ago. They had even started to work out Nicole's schedule so it wouldn't interfere with her last month of school. And of course, she found out with the rest of us this morning that Kelly was given the job a month ago so she put in her two-week notice this morning.

"I think it'll be fine. The deadline isn't until Friday," I assured her.

"Oh, that's good. I don't know what happened. I just spaced. I swear, I'm such a retard."

"No, it's really okay," I insisted.

She had just knocked herself out, and she hadn't even entered the ring. Was that her way of winning the fight of admitting her mistakes—calling herself stupid and retarded? Obviously, she had misunderstood the rope a dope. How did she expect to make a comeback from her mistakes and knock out adversity when she was helping the opposition?

colored adolescence

Later at lunch . . .

Yeah, it took them a while, but I finally started getting lunch invitations again.

Lisa had decided that a few of us should have a welcome lunch for Kelly since it was her first day, even though it took them a couple of months to even invite me to a lunch.

"I'm so fat! I look disgusting!" Lisa confessed.

"I know, every time I look in the mirror, it's so gross," Miranda added.

"Have you guys heard about that new protein diet?" Kelly asked.

It was my turn and I had nothing. The four of us were sitting eating lunch. The three of them were nibbling on salads and I was wolfing down a cheeseburger. Don't ask me why. Their sizes combined were still smaller than my size twelve. But their obsession with depriving themselves of the nourishment of self-esteem and self-love prohibited them from tasting anything mouthwatering. They were used to substitutions because they had grown up eating tofu esteem.

What did they want me to say? "Because I don't have the body of a manufactured supermodel, I'm the most disgusting creature on the face of the earth?" Please! I know I'm beautiful 'cause my mama taught me that the same time she was teaching me my ABC's. It wasn't a difficult formula to memorize, but they had trouble with the simple calculation because they had spent their lives trying to master the more complex ones such as adding calories, subtracting self-worth, multiplying outer beauty, and dividing self-love into the square root of society. And remember this was the same group who couldn't add and divide the food bill the last time we went to lunch together.

"Hmm, this may be the best burger I've ever had."

What? That's all I had!

"Oh, I don't even want to think about what a burger would do to me," Lisa said.

Maybe fill you up?

"I know. Especially since my vacation is coming up. I need to get into my new bikini in two weeks. I forgot to tell you guys that I bought it last week. It was really expensive but hopefully it will pay off in Cancun. It's so hot! Maybe I'll meet my husband," Miranda planned.

Like it had been impossible to get into one last year being a big size two.

"I don't even want to think about a bikini. I really need to get some sun. I'm so pale," Lisa complained.

"You should try this tanning salon I go to. It's great!" Kelly offered.

"I'm all into the bronzers. They really work," Miranda suggested.

Well, at least I haven't been missing much the months that I've been banned from lunches.

"Oh, I still think you should check out the salon," Kelly said.

Yeah, I still have nothing to contribute to the conversation.

"That was a huge salad!" Lisa said.

"I know, I'm so stuffed," Miranda agreed.

As they finished the last bite of their half-eaten, regular-size salad, I begin to wonder how they could not be hungry. But I guess after stuffing their face with society's perception of beautiful, they were addicted to throwing up the real source of protein for their health. I wish I had even thought about throwing up food that my mama had worked so hard to put on the table. Forget slowly killing

colored adolescence

myself because Mama would have done it after my first thought.

After their light meals, they begin the process of creating their tofu beauty while concealing their natural self to the world. It's absolutely amazing at the number of makeup and skin products that are on the market these days. Their daily makeup bags were filled with everything—from eye wrinkle gel to bronzers. And they wonder why they look sixty at forty.

"Do you ever wear makeup?" Kelly asked.

"Yeah, come to think of it, I never see you in makeup," Miranda noticed.

Probably because I don't need it.

"I wear lipstick and that's about it unless I'm going out," I answered.

"Well, you have such beautiful skin. You really don't have to, I guess," Kelly said.

"Yeah, it's so smooth. You have great skin," Lisa said.

It's funny; I had never been complimented on my skin before I entered their world. I guess it's not a big deal when everyone in your circle is a Nubian beauty queen wearing the same crown. You just don't stand out. No one is trying to inject blackness in their lips or project pigment in their shade because everyone just acknowledges their royal blessings.

"Thanks."

"Can I touch it?" Lisa asked.

Like I really want your dirty hands in my face.

"Uh, I guess."

"It's so smooth. It's like caramel. What type of products do you use?" she asked.

None of the crap in your bags.

"Cocoa butter."

"That's it?" Miranda asked.
"Yep, that's it."
"Wow!" they all said in unison.

Sometimes simple is better. Mama taught me that. We never had fifty moisturizers for normal to dry or dry to oily skin in our house. Everyone had Vaseline-type skin. Mama would spread it on so thick that even Ali couldn't connect a punch. Maybe that's the problem. Maybe we need more champs of self-esteem—you know parents who can train and teach their little girls that they are the greatest regardless of their weigh-in or opponents. Don't get me wrong. We all diet. We all have our days of personal insecurities and society's expectations. I mean I was feeling a little out of place during the entire lunch of weight worries, tanning conversations and makeup applications. But at the end of the day, it seems that we're most likely to last all twelve rounds. Regardless of the punches and jabs, we're able to pick ourselves back up and prepare to get back into the ring the next day with our floating endurance and stinging confidence.

You know, I've been trying to be quiet and just sit back, observe, and do as I'm told. But, I'm finding each day I'm developing a dislike for this place. No matter how much I try, I'm just not fitting in here. They wonder why we're so disgruntled. It's not because of perceived prejudices. Has anyone ever thought what coming to work every day and not being able to identify with the people around you can do to you? It's hard not being able to discuss the new black sitcom on UPN or the new Bebe Moore Campbell book. For some reason, I can't get fully comfortable in this place. And only I can feel it. I really don't have anything in common, at least anything that really matters, with these people. We think different. Our backgrounds are different.

colored adolescence

Our preferences are different. Our actions are different. We're just different, and nothing can change that. How is this fair? What can I do to feel better? How can I cure my loneliness? What is my purpose? How can this be the life that I've worked so hard to live?

colored adolescence

July 25

Dear Diary,

I knew it was too good to be true. Why is that every time you sit down to relax and get comfortable with something, another something always knocks on the door of your established home? And unlike the average solicitor, it doesn't just walk away when no one answers or give up when the house suddenly goes from well lit to pitch dark. Instead, it lingers until you ultimately need to step out for a breath of fresh air. And that's when it somehow forces its way into your everyday life.

Sometimes it can be difficult to depend entirely on your individuality because of constant peer pressure. Even though you're focused to remain on your path, other side roads constantly tempt you to stray for a more enjoyable and faster journey. That can be a difficult decision when you see the majority taking shortcuts instead of their own unique path. You begin to think that maybe giving up the scenic route, even though it captures some of your favorite pictures of the road trips, isn't so bad. You also start to envy those labeled as the "intelligent" travelers and wish you could travel smart too. And that's the hard part. You somehow know that no matter how many shortcuts you take, you'll still be looked at as the one who copied the skillful travelers' route. Ultimately, you just continue to travel on your personal deserted highway and get to destinations by using your own detailed map.

My workplace family is having a hard time accepting my colored adolescence and letting go of the negro, independent child that they have admired since its nigger birth. They disapprove of my individual way of thinking and expression because they think that it isn't proper for a teenager to behave so maturely. The childlike ways were cute but my budding grown-up tendencies are threatening. They want to keep me as a child for as long as they possibly can. That way I can't do any harm. As a child, I didn't have to learn how to drive my own car. I couldn't go out without their supervision. I could just remain a cute little kid with impressive abilities that they could brag about to the neighbors. But you can't stop growth.

So instead of joining my civil rights protests, they remain on the other side of the picket lines. I don't really mind because I have met others who are going through the same movement so I'm not entirely alone. But I do feel

colored adolescence

like I am moving backward instead of growing forward. No matter how hard I try to drive my own style to my destiny, they always find reasons for me to pull over at a rest stop. But I am never going to rest.

black adulthood

August 9

Dear Diary,

Being grown is harder than I thought it would be. I have to fight more now to keep my freedom than I did to gain it. Once I defeated my first battle, I had a responsibility to prove that I not only deserved independence, but I could cultivate it into something positive and rewarding. But as I am learning, some do not take defeat well. So eventually, other small wars started to constantly bombard my land. Suddenly, there are more temptations that insist on seizing my free will. And there are established minds stuck on challenging my ability to nurture my independence. So, I have no other choice but to fight back. And of course, once I start to rebel and sniff victory, I am labeled as an aggressive dictator who cares only about my self-gain.

    I am constantly trying to figure out what I could have done to prepare for the war of adulthood in my adolescence. I thought I had done everything right by accepting what is instead of what should be. I have outgrown the tantrums and fights. I have ceased my high expectations of utopia. I have even stopped keeping a daily diary because I felt that it was something that adults just didn't do. But there are some things that you just can't be told or shown. Some things you just have to experience for yourself. And being an adult is one of them. No one can prepare you to make the difficult decisions that can possibly change everything. No one can tell you how to win some of the drawn-out battles that will end up on your territory. You just have to learn as you fight. And that's what I'm doing. There are many times that my enemies attempt to surprise me with another vicious attack. There are days where I am ready to surrender to the unpredictable obstacles. My passion is constantly being tested, and my hunger is questioned. How bad do you want this? What are you willing to sacrifice? Didn't we just feed you a bland meal? How much will it take to satisfy your appetite?

When I finally received the freedom that I had anxiously been seeking since I was old enough to dream, I was relieved and overjoyed. I was grown! It had taken long enough. I thought, this was it! There was no stopping my success because I had my goals, I had my passion and I had my attack plan; I was ready to conquer the world. I felt that victory was guaranteed because I had endured so many hardships and setbacks and had yet to give up. I deserved to win the ultimate war, right? Yeah, life doesn't quite work like that.

free at last, thank god almighty, i'm free at last!

October 30

Dear Diary,

Have you ever heard of a party starting on time? And if you have, have you ever heard of anyone getting there on time? And if you have, why didn't anyone tell me? I know that we don't have the greatest record of promptness but I thought parties were an exception. Everybody knows that one should arrive fashionably late to any soiree. So, when I read that our company's Halloween party started at 7:30 p.m., I assumed that I would arrive on time, 8:30 p.m. But then you had to account for C.P. (colored people) time so

40 Hours and an Unwritten Rule

I got there at 9:00 p.m. I guess I was the only one who interpreted the invite that way.

But I'm convinced that we have some sort of gene that forces us to believe that it's an hour earlier than it really is when it comes to any event. It's because of this disorder that I'm usually late to everything.

1. Church
   (do they still do devotion?)
2. Hair appointments
   (they take all day anyway)
3. Work
   (but I'm salaried)
4. Graduations
   (yep, even to my own)
5. Funerals
   (unless I'm part of the family)
6. Holiday celebrations
   (my family never starts anything on time)
7. Parties
   (but that's normal, isn't it?)

Maybe this trait was passed down from generation to generation. You know, it probably started after emancipation. After years of having to live and work by the master's time, can you blame black folks for creating our own?

When I made my grand entrance in the restaurant, I

adulthood in black

felt the illusory spotlight shift from the dance floor to the front door where I was standing. I had decided to dress up as a black cat. And of course, I had my evening look going: alluring makeup, fresh hairdo, a sexy, but classy cat suit. *Meooooow!* But did that deserve the limelight? As I looked around the room, I suddenly realized that the party had already reached its climax and was now fighting the conclusion. I looked at my watch—9:27 p.m.

Okay, so I was a little late, but the party couldn't be over! I was suppose to get there right around the time when everyone had loosened up and was tired of playing the bullshit party politics game. People were done kissing bosses' asses and the square employees had already called it a night. It was supposed to be the climax, the time where the alcoholics had drank so much that even they were wasted and people finally didn't care if everyone saw that they didn't have rhythm. People were ready to partay! All of this usually occurs no later than two hours into the night. I mean, it was supposed to be a company soiree, wasn't it? But again, I guess I was the only one who had interpreted the evening's schedule that way.

Now that it was apparent that I was so late that I had missed Brenden's "thank you for a great year" speech and more importantly the party itself, I had to come up with a good excuse for my tardiness. I knew I was about to get bombarded with "Why are you so late?" from everyone who had noticed my absence, which would be all of their nosy asses. And since I was as noticeable as a straight male in a gay nightclub, I was expecting to hear that question for the rest of the evening.

I knew that my excuse not only had to be good enough to justify me missing a company function, but also good enough to make me look admirable. So, I ruled out the real reason, the Lifetime movie that I had seen twice before but couldn't remember who actually did "it." So,

40 Hours and an Unwritten Rule

I had to see the last court scene where they exonerated the suspected killer and revealed the real murderer. But I couldn't let them know that a Lifetime Original was more important than Brenden's ego-driven speech. Could I?

"We were looking for you. Why are you so late?" Lisa asked.

Not that's it's any of their business but...

"Oh, I had another Halloween party tonight," I confessed. "I didn't realize it was going to go so long."

Ok, we've all done it at one point or another. The only difference is that usually it's done the other way around. You know how you're at a boring party and need an excuse to go home. So what do you do? "Oh, I have to stop by another party on my way home."

With this excuse, I not only implied that this party was more important than my own company's party by arriving late rather than skipping or bailing out on the first one, but I'd built my reputation as someone who gets invited to important parties. And you know I can't be more important than they are. So you already know the next question...

"What was this other party?" she asked.

Remember, keep them guessing.

"Oh, I'll tell you about it later. I need a drink."

Don't worry, she will tell everybody and they all will find a way to ask again.

As I was walking toward the bar...

"Hey. You finally made it. I know that you're probably a great dancer. Let's dance!" Amy screamed.

Before I knew it, I was dancing to some hip-hop song. I was trying hard to tune out what my eyes were seeing so I could keep myself on beat. But every time I looked anywhere but up, I found myself as lost as a slave who had just been freed. I was struggling to get a piece of my own land, but the master kept holding me down to labor his rhythmless field. I finally spotted Craig and Derek at the other end of the dance floor and smoothly started to ditch Amy.

But then it happened. You know how you have your song? The song that was meant for you to dance to over and over? A song that is so connected to your soul that it feels like you gave birth to every word and beat. Yeah, we all have at least one of those. So, when I heard "my song," I was free! Suddenly, I didn't need alcohol to loosen me up or a group of people to take attention away from me. I stepped off to the side on my own land and began to move. I just needed "my song" to capture my freedom. My feet began to move faster than the furious feet that had chased our strong men through the dark woods. My hips were moving to a beat louder than that of the lustful souls who had controlled our beautiful women. My powerful arms began to swing back at all the aggressive arms that had swung their wild whips at our innocent children. I was in control and no one could cage my rhythm.

After feeling the music for a couple of songs, my feet started to move to the side, two, three, four and the other side, two, three, four and back two, three, four, and dip . . . Heeeeey! I was grooving the Harlem Shuffle and of course, Craig and Derek followed. Come on, it *is* a party.

Okay, I forgot where I was.

I started to feel like us black folks were giving a show because a crowd had formed around the dance floor 'cause the three of us were jammin'. And of course, some were rocking one side with the music and the other half was feeling it to the opposite side. And then there were some who, I guess, kept forgetting which side they had just rocked to and were repeating the side for the second time.

After the fourth song, I finally noticed the fans cheering for our freedom. But then it hit me . . . we were giving a benefit concert—a free show to our captors. Although the crowd was filled with disabled dancers, the last thing any of these people needed was charity. I abruptly ended the show and spent the rest of the night answering questions at a nearby table with my dignity keeping me company. I kept getting the same questions all night:

"Wow! I didn't know you could move like that!"

"What do you call that dance you were doing?"

"You look so beautiful with makeup!"

Like we can't play dress-up too . . .

"You're such a great dancer!"

"Why were you so late?"

"You look just like the teacher in Fame out there!"

"You look amazing tonight."

"You have to teach me to dance like that."

"So, what other party did you go to tonight?"

"When are you going to get back on the dance floor?"

"Where were you earlier?"

"Come on, you have to show me that dance."

"Why were you so late?"

After I escaped all of the questions and requests for dance lessons, I began to understand how the great performers like Dorothy, Sammy, or Josephine felt after they, too, had gained their freedom on stage. What a feeling! But all good things must come to an end, so, I said my good-byes and tapped my way home.

I actually had fun tonight. This is what it is, and I just have to stop harping on the situation because it's not going to change. This is life! Tonight, I decided that I'm going to stop complaining. If I don't like it then it's up to me to change it. So, what's the lesson learned tonight?

1. Never get on a dance floor with anyone who thinks that the Harlem Shuffle is a card game originated in Harlem.

2. Don't dance in heels that are not made for dancing.

3. To avoid extra attention, don't substantiate the stereotype that we can't get anywhere on time. (I'm not saying throw out your C.P. watch, just don't wear it to company functions.)

raid!

November 25

Dear Diary,

It was just one of those days. I had been anticipating the arrival of today since the first time I turned the key in the lock of my new home and it finally crept in this afternoon. You know the saying, "Things happen when you least expect them?" That is so, so true. I mean, I thought that I had finally settled into my space. I had even been thinking about renewing my lease.

But today, it happened—the bugs finally came out and crawled freely around the office. And they didn't even wait until the lights were turned off. They stampeded out in full daylight. I had never seen anything like it. They didn't care that I was standing in the same room with them. They weren't making an effort to hide their presence. What was I supposed to do?

These roaches were so bold and swift that I'm not even sure that Raid could take care of the infestation problem that took over today. I was caught completely off guard 'cause I know that I don't keep a nasty house, but I guess when you have messy neighbors, it's only a matter of time before they make their way to your space.

"I think we should target minorities," Adam suggested.

Great idea!

I was in my first official meeting with the bigwigs. I had gotten a pseudo promotion as a coordinator without the elevated title or pay. But I wasn't bothered by it too much because I knew it wasn't a personal or race thing; these people were just cheap, unethical bastards. So I was invited to this meeting because of some special project that I'd been assigned (well, I guess we now know that it was probably the minority-targeted one). So far, I was agreeing with what I was hearing—target minorities. See I knew they cared a little bit.

"Yeah, that's a great idea. We would look like the heroes because no one else is doing it right now," Kathy responded.

Hey, we all know it's always all about them so if we can squeeze in their limelight, it's okay 'cause we both shine, right?

"That's a great idea. Your department will work together to present a plan," Adam instructed.

While he was saying "your department" to Kathy, he was looking at the department, me. Of course, I'm going to be selected for anything "minority related" but I'm not trippin'; at least it'll be done right because you know I'm going to represent!

"What groups are we trying to target?" Kathy asked.

"I think it should be all of them—African-Americans, Hispanics, Asians, Native-Americans," Brenden answered.

Sure! Just group us all together.

"Okay, I'll have a report by the end of the week," Kathy responded.

"How!"

Everyone turned to look at Adam. Huh?

"How!"

"What?" everyone responded.

"How! Get it?"

As Adam said, "get it," he raised his right hand by his face.

Yeah, I got it. But did he get the diversity tape that he was forced to watch on his first day?

The room, with the exception of me, exploded in laughter. I began to wonder if any of them had watched the tape. Was it just a requirement for minorities? I don't understand.

"Okay, let's get back to business," Adam said, laughing. Gordon, can you summarize your finance report?"

"I don't know. I have some reservations about that," Gordon Bornstein in Finance said. "Get it?"

The room once again exploded in laughter.

I'm not feeling this. Is this what goes on every week? Maybe that's why they haven't hired any minority high-level executives 'cause the jokes would always be on them in these meetings.

"Okay, okay," Adam said as he tried to bring the

room to the order. "Moving on. So, let's focus now on upper-class African-Americans."

"Upper-class African-Americans? That's not realistic," Gordon shouted.

Oprah, Colin Powell, Johnnie Cochran, Robert Johnson, John Johnson, Bill Cosby, Maya, Condoleezza, Susan Taylor, Denzel, Halle, Will and Jada, Michael Jordan, Spike Lee . . .

I was facing a dilemma. Should I or shouldn't I? This was my first time sitting in on their weekly informal meeting. And after all, they saw it as being just between family; if you can't trust family, then who can you trust? I was just a fly on the wall. Although I was wishing that I could transform into a bee so I could sting all their tactless asses.

But if I made my presence known, would they squash me with their bare hands? Or would they force me out by just swooshing me out of their window of opportunity. Or was it possible that they would allow my strong buzz to stay and live among them in peace?

"Well, I know, but let's just use the few that exist," Adam agreed.

Magic, Russell Simmons, Michael Jackson, Janet Jackson, Cathy Hughes, Tiger Woods, P. Diddy, Dick Parsons . . .

"We need to decide where we can target these African-Americans so we can build the campaign," Kathy suggested.

"What about Beverly Hills?" Adam suggested.

"That's a great idea," Kathy responded.

"Beverly Hills? You mean Baldwin Hills!" Gordon shouted, talking about a black community in Los Angeles.

Had I died and come back as a ghost without

knowing it? That was the only excuse I had for them not seeing and acknowledging me sitting in the chair in the back of the room.

The room exploded in more laughter.

"Okay, we've gotten ourselves into enough trouble today."

As Adam said "trouble," he glanced over my way. My eyes were shouting, "Damn right, there have to be consequences for your offensive actions."

What's wrong with these people? Why are they so ignorant? Why are they so arrogant? Why are they so indifferent? Why do they think they're so invulnerable?

I began to wonder about the consequences of my desired counterattack. Should I speak up? If I spoke up would I be fired and have my name placed on the FBI's Ten Most Wanted list? Was I going to be framed for other crimes that I had not committed? Would they try to make an example out of me by showing everyone that speaking up for right would lead you to meet a wrong path? Would they disown me and ban me from future family gatherings? Would I be labeled as the black sheep of the family with petty issues? After asking these questions over and over in my mind, I finally realized that I wasn't demanding much. It wasn't like I was trying to enforce a ten-point plan; I just wanted one—I Want Respect. That's all this was about. I didn't care if they genuinely felt that way or if they were joking. It didn't matter if these types of jokes were just normal conversation among family or if they only surfaced today because of the topic of this week's meeting. I didn't give a damn who said what or what title that person held. They were all guilty of disrespect, and they had to be chastised. Hey, just because their mamas hadn't done it didn't mean I couldn't.

As I looked around the room at the ignorant hecklers,

I became enraged. Who did these people think they were? Could I disrespect Adam and go on without being reprimanded? Would I be allowed to disgrace the Caucasian race and have the room remain silent? I don't think so.

But I also knew that I couldn't get down on the floor and crawl around with them. Not only did I not want to be mistaken for another creepy crawler; I just don't get down like that. I had no desire to search for used jokes that had been thrown in the trash years ago. And I didn't want to mate with any these bold creatures to lay eggs of hatred and ignorance.

I just wanted to nip this problem in the bud and continue to live bug free. And I knew that putting traps down would not only take too long, but could possibly miss the capture of every little bug. It was time to spray their asses with something toxic and effective. I needed something strong but something that wouldn't leave that stinky smell throughout the house. I was forced to excuse myself and leave the office so I could whip up a deadly potion that would exterminate their disrespect.

So, you know when you make a resolution and say you're going to work out at the beginning of the year, and never go to the gym? Well, look at my promise to stop complaining as my resolution that was made to be broken 'cause this is bullshit! How can I let this go?

What did I do to freakin' deserve this? Maybe Eve was black. That's the only possible excuse that would explain why I have to go through this shit! What was the point of the Civil Rights Movement, or Martin, or Malcolm, or affirmative action if we still have to sit in on this? Was it all in vain? Will these people ever get it? I've tried to adapt. I've tried to ignore. I even sampled white chocolate—briefly! But nothing seems to be enough for these people! What more can I fuckin' do to make myself feel at home?

I can't even describe the anger and hurt I'm feeling right now. I hate them! This is worst than being in love. How could these people betray me like that? How could they cheat right in front of my face and not even care if they got caught? After that meeting, I was so mad I couldn't look at them for the rest of the day. So, after telling Craig and Derek, I went home ill 'cause I was sick of them and all of the diseased shit that they passed around today.

tag! you're it!

November 26

Adam,

    I wanted to express how appalled I was after the meeting yesterday. I felt many uncomfortable moments during the entire meeting. From the Native-American jokes to the "Baldwin Hills" reference, I felt I was disrespected as a minority more than once. My first thought was to ignore my feelings because I would seem too sensitive or be looked at as an overreacting employee; however, when I went back to my desk, I still felt just as uncomfortable. When I got home last night, again, those same feelings remained with me. My feelings are "my" feelings. That's when I knew that no matter how irrelevant and harmless the comments were to others, they were still offensive to me, so they mattered. And I had a responsibility to myself to express how the meeting made me feel.

    I think certain people in the room didn't really take a moment to think about how things were said. I understand that we are a small, close-knit group; however, there still has to be some form of professionalism when discussing certain topics such as race-related issues, especially when a minority is present. As a minority in all of my workplace environments in the *past, I have learned to overlook certain slips of the tongue. After all, we all make jokes at others' expense when we're not around those groups. However, when certain people are present, people should be respectful and mindful of those comments. And with the room being diverse with other minorities, such as Jews and homosexuals, I was surprised to hear some of the jokes that were made.*

I guess I am writing this email to just bring it to your attention. I don't need any apologies or further action. Apparently you felt something was wrong because of your comment after the "Baldwin Hills" joke regarding getting yourself into enough trouble. Since I'm not involved in every meeting, I'm not sure if this is a common practice that goes on weekly. As a matter of fact, it wouldn't bother me if it were. I understand that as a lower-level employee, sometimes you get snubbed and in this case are supposed to be an observer. However, as a human being, I expect just as much respect as any executive sitting in one of the chairs at the table. Therefore, when I sit in on meetings in the future, I would appreciate if others would refrain from certain comments and jokes and recognize that although they may find them to be harmless humor that they're laughing at someone else's expense. Thanks!

After writing the email, I had doubts. Craig and Derek both loved it. Mama thought it was too soft. And the people on the south side wanted me to add some of their complaints at the end. But I was still going back and forth about my letter. Would it seem like I was overly sensitive by holding unnecessary grudges? I mean why couldn't I just get over it? By pressing the send button could I possibly be clicking on negative perceptions of my neighbors? Would they perceive me as the militant, angry black girl instead of the quiet neighbor who had the well-manicured lawn? Would everyone stop inviting me to lunches and drinks after work in fear that I was on a mission to extract information for my rebellious war? Would residents feel threatened by my presence?

But then I started to think. They had tagged me. I have to admit; they caught me fair and square. I had become too comfortable and confident of my place in the family. I had slowed down because I assumed I was safe. There were estranged cousins who had come after me; therefore, I thought that my proven loyalty had somehow bumped me up to be viewed as any other blood relative in the household. But I guess I was wrong. So, I couldn't just stop the game; I refuse to let them win that easy. I not only had to run after my pride, but I had to sprint to catch their ignorant, condescending asses.

By choosing the delete button, I was not only deleting the email, but throwing years of perseverance and hard work in the trash. I wasn't going to let years of killings, months of marches, days of boycotts and minutes of speeches dissolve in a second. I had to remind them that just because we had stopped crying for them to embrace us as equals didn't mean we were going to settle for a handshake of respect. I had no choice, so I hit "send email." It didn't matter that I had attached myself to some of these people. It was time to say good-bye. I had to kiss whatever consequences would appear in my face good-bye and greet my dignity with a welcoming smile.

merry christmas

December 23

Dear Diary,

Christmas has always been my favorite time of the year. Colorful lights. Pine smells. Traditional carols. Wrapped presents. Holiday cheer. But this year, I'm just in a funk—They have stolen my joy. But last night I decided that I'm not going to let these people ruin my holiday. So I decided to share my richness and enjoy the spirit of giving.

"Merry Christmas."
As I handed Kathy the red envelope, I couldn't help but to smile and rejoice in the moment. This was the first time since my email situation that I had felt delight in this place. A couple of days after Adam sent his pretentious email apology, Brandi in HR sat me down and talked with me about my happiness and needs with the company. Of

course Adam had contacted Brandi right after he received my email to cover his butt. After assuring Brandi that I wasn't going to take further action, certain executives had become overly nice to me. Kathy had a new respect and fear of me because she had never seen anyone stand up to Adam. Brenden had even added a smile to his good morning greeting.

As Kathy removed the Christmas card from the envelope, she was speechless. She searched for words but her blank expression said it all. She hadn't even bothered to open the card before she decided to thank me.

"Oh, I mean, thank you, Racey. What a nice card," she said.

I wasn't going to push it. So I just said, "You're welcome."

Suddenly, I had regained my misplaced holiday spirit. As I walked down the hall passing out my Christmas cards, I realized that all this time it wasn't me. It was them. The different reactions to a stupid Christmas card revealed all of their guilty thoughts.

"Oh, how cute," Lisa said as she removed her card from the envelope.

Lisa couldn't find any other words from her usually large vocabulary.

"That's something the way the little black doll is dressed in a Santa costume," she continued.

Well, I wasn't counting on that particular response from my ethnic Christmas cards but leave it to them to surprise me every time. To tell you the truth, I wasn't really expecting any response. It was just a card. When I saw them at the store last night, I bought them because I was tired of conforming to be like them. I just wanted something that embraced who I am and the cards with a black Santa and black kids were the closest thing. I wanted them to know that I wasn't ashamed of my culture and I no longer had a desire to deny it.

The rest of the office did their best to not cross my path for the rest of the day. Those who needed my help every day before today, suddenly gained a new independence and handled the work by themselves or just emailed me their questions and requests. But that was fine with me. Their silence was a treasured gift on its own.

But you know that there has to be at least one to break the enjoyed silence. Earlier in the day, Amy, along with everyone else, had sent me an email request. And after I responded, she felt the need to break the silence and make herself comfortable with me again.

Racey,
Thanks for the information, sista—or is it girlfriend?

Well, nothing lasts forever. But it felt good to watch them be uncomfortable for once, even if it was for a couple of hours.

shut up, mother!

January 13

Dear Diary,

There are some things you just can't get away with in this world.

1. First-degree murder
   (punishable with the death sentence)
2. Three strikes
   (punishable with life in prison)
3. The most dreadful of them all:
   A child cursing his mother
   (punishable with a slow, painful death with eternity in hell)

I didn't realize that this law didn't pertain to all children and all mothers until this afternoon. Who knew? Before today, I couldn't imagine that a human could put himself through that unpredictable torture. But before this morning, I also didn't realize that the laws of the household were like the laws of the court; some people, depending on who you are, can get away with murder.

"You're so fuckin' stupid! Why are you being so fuckin' difficult?"

What did the person do? Was it really that bad? I wasn't straining to hear every crude word that Jeff Baker was screaming into his telephone two cubicles down from me. Boy, he was really upset! This was unlike him because he was always in a good mood. I was hoping that it was a guy on the other end of the conversation because I couldn't imagine a sane woman taking that degree of abuse. It was so bad that I was wondering if a fist would have felt better than the painful words that he was spewing.

"I don't care what you bought!" Jeff shouted. "I told you that I couldn't fuckin' make it! God, why do you have to act so stupid sometimes? . . . How can I do that? . . . If I couldn't do it a week ago, what makes you think I can do it today? . . . You're acting like a child . . . Hey, you're the one who's acting like a retard! Why would you spend the goddamn money if you're going to be such a bitch about it? . . . Look, I'm at work. I can't talk about this right now . . . Just shut up, you're acting silly right now."

Oh, so he just realized that he's at work and that, not only does he not have an office where he can close his door, but that his foul language is inappropriate for a professional environment? What was taking Kathy so long to approach his cubicle to reprimand him on his behavior? Clearly, this was a personal call. Hell, she found the time to confront me about my scarf that she had mistaken for a baseball cap.

Jeff continued, "Look, I will talk to you later. I don't have time for you right now because you're acting stupid. I'm hanging up! I'm not kidding, I'm hanging up! Goodbye, Mother!"

Mother? As in Mom? Like Mommy? As in the person who went through hours of excruciating labor to bring you into this world?

The phone and my mouth dropped at the same time, with the same force. I started to get nervous just thinking about what would've happened if my tongue had gotten up the nerve to belt out those words to my mother. Just the thought of the repercussions was worse than stage fright. Was he not afraid? Was he invincible? Was it his "real" mother or maybe just a friend whose nickname was Mother? I had to get to the bottom of this. Okay, call me nosy but I had to see for myself if this was possible.

Still fearing for his life, I nervously walked to Jeff's cubicle. I didn't want to be caught in the crossfire of whatever punishment he was about to experience. I was wondering why his mother hadn't made her way through the phone to choke all of those hateful words from his mouth. I know mine would have found a way. But I was overreacting because I just knew it couldn't have been his real mother, right?

"Are you alright?" I asked.

Yes, I was playing the concerned coworker. Hey, they do it to me all the time.

"Yeah, my mother can be so dumb sometimes."
"You mean your real mother?"
"Yeah. She lives in Maryland," he answered.
I immediately took a couple of steps back because

I didn't want any confusion as to who God was coming after. I know it wasn't any of my business, but I continued interrogating him because justice had to prevail.

"So, she lets you talk to her like that?" I pressured.

"Like what?"

"You know, like she's some guy in a bar."

"What? She made me mad. She bought me a ticket to come home next weekend for my aunt's funeral after I told her that I couldn't get off work. And now she's complaining that she wasted her money on the ticket."

Now I know the result of the little white five-year-old boy who tells his mother no while having a tantrum in the checkout line at the grocery store.

"But don't you think that it's wrong to disrespect your own mother like that?" I questioned.

"I wasn't disrespecting her! It's not like I called her the c-word or anything. And she deserved it! If she acted like she had common sense, I wouldn't get so upset."

"Wow! There is no way that I could ever talk to my mother like that. I wouldn't even go there if I'm talking to someone in her presence. She's okay with you talking to her like that?"

"She knows that I was upset."

"And so the next time you see her, nothing is going to happen to you?"

"Like what?"

"My mother would kill me!"

"Why?"

"Because she's my mother," I explained.

"And? What do you do when she makes you upset?"

"Call my friends and tell them that she made me upset. That is just somewhere that I don't have the option of going with my mother."

I realized that nothing I was going to say was going to

change his way of communicating with his mother. Was it a white thing? But I had been around other white people who wouldn't dare disrespect their mother like he had done. And I knew white parents who would have skipped the lethal injection process and would have taken pleasure in killing their child with their bare hands. I know that anything's possible, but damn, this was unimaginable with a black child and a black mother.

I had always looked at my mother as if she was the second god (if there was such a thing) on earth. She gave me life; she had molded me into the person I am today. Even though our relationship hadn't always been perfect, it was impossible for me to take any of that away from her with disrespecting words. But his mother had told him that it was okay by not slapping him in the mouth the first time he even thought some of those blasphemous words. So, I knew that I couldn't convince him of converting to my beliefs when his mother had instilled her own religion in him. But I was still annoyed, confused, and angry that he could get away with it. He could just walk away unaffected by his crime with not even a slap on the wrist. He was free to do whatever he wanted without facing any punishments for his repulsive acts. God bless America!

when is black history month?

February 10

Dear Diary,

Do you think while some people are destined to be great, others are destined to remain insignificant? And while some people are destined to grow, others are meant to remain rooted? Maybe there always has to be a balance. But why do some people tip the scale? Why is it that while some people learn, other people continue to harbor ignorance in their mind when it comes to other cultures' achievements and contributions to society?

"What are you doing this weekend?" Matt asked. Since our lunch, he sometimes acted funny but every now and then he would strike up conversation with me. So I guess we were still cool.

"I have to rehearse for a program I'm doing with my sorority for Black History Month," I answered.

"Oh, when is Black History Month?"

Huh?

I don't know why it surprised me that Matt didn't know, but I was still shocked by the lack of knowledge on his part. I mean he graduated from Yale. It's amazing how white people boast and brag on their high-level education and their renaissance knowledge, but they're illiterate when it comes to reading the history of our culture. He probably didn't even know it was an entire month.

"It's this month," I answered.

"What day?"

Okay, I was really kidding about him not knowing that it was an entire month. It's funny, as usual we got the short end of the stick when they generously gave us the shortest month of the entire year, and yet they're still trying to shorten it. Now, I'm not only bothered but I'm a little upset. I understand that he probably didn't grow up reciting famous speeches or singing spiritual songs of faith and hope of our past and present, but he could at least rejoice high enough for the children of our weary ancestors to reach.

"It's the entire month."

Hence, Black History Month.

"Oh, that's right. I forgot about that. So what do you actually do?" he asked.

"When?"

"You know, when you celebrate."

I explained, "We just remember all of those before us who have made a contribution and a difference. And not just in our lives but everybody's daily life."

"Who is there besides Martin Luther King and that Rosa Parks woman?" he insisted.

"What do you mean?"

"Like are there enough famous black people to make a month of it?" he asked, shrugging.

You can't fight ignorance with anger . . .

"Actually there are enough to make a year," I boasted.

"Oh, who knew? I wonder why there isn't a white history month. There's a lot of famous white people who have made contributions to society."

Maybe that's because they have stolen everybody's ideas and have claimed them as their own.

But remember you can't fight ignorance with anger . . . you can't fight ignorance with anger.

"You should come to our program."

Okay, hurry up and make up an excuse.

"Oh, I would love to, but I already have plans."

But I didn't tell you the date.

"That's too bad. It's going to be a great show."

You wonder. They celebrate and enjoy other holidays that they weren't one hundred percent responsible for creating. They eat on Thanksgiving. They drink on St. Patrick's Day. They kiss on Valentine's Day. So, why can't they pull up a chair and partake in the nourishment of our ancestors, the buzz of our talents, and the slobber of contributions that we have generously given to them in spite of the endless barriers that they have kindheartedly given to us? Maybe it's because they will be forced to study the vast achievements we have made without their instruction. Maybe it's because they don't want to memorize the guilt of their part in our ongoing struggle. Maybe it's because they will comprehend our incredible strength that has continuously broken their unyielding chains. Maybe they know that they will finally have to give us the credits we've earned and then we'll be forced to graduate from their institutions of life. And then they will be forced to acknowledge our degrees of independence and brilliance.

For some reason, they would just rather become delinquent when it comes to any form of education of our history. Perhaps, they don't have a desire to learn because they feel that they would never use it in the real world. Would they be tested on it when they apply for a job? Could there be a possibility that it could ever be coffee table conversation? Would people within their circles be impressed by their black history knowledge? Probably not. So why bother?

It's not like they had to sign their name with their fountain pens throughout their busy days at work. And it's not like they couldn't take the stairs instead of stepping into the elevator to leave for the day in their automatic gearshift cars. And while driving to their air-conditioned homes, it wasn't likely that they would have to stop at a traffic light or get held up by a slow street sweeper picking up all their clutter. I mean, chances were slim that they would even need to cut their overgrown grass with their lawn mower. They probably wouldn't need to mop their kitchen floor that was full of dirt tracked from their favorite pair of shoes, that surprisingly they had worn for years, getting muddy from the wet grass watered with the lawn sprinkler. And certainly they wouldn't even think about opening their refrigerator to take out the jelly to make a peanut butter and jelly sandwich to satisfy their full stomachs because they didn't need anymore food of knowledge to complement their diet.

Yeah, it's not like black history has impacted their lives.

old habits are hard to break

February 21

Dear Diary,

Everyone has that thing they do. There are people who smoke under pressure. Other people stutter when they lie. Some people bite their nails when they're nervous. We all have a habit of some kind. Some are harmless while others are dangerous. Some are cute and others are distasteful. Then there are those that are tolerable and those that are just annoying as hell. What is it with white women and their hair? Why can't they go longer than a knock-knock joke without messing with their tresses? It doesn't matter if it's shoulder-length or just above the chin. They will run their fingers through it, put it up and put it back down, all within a simple conversation. Damn the person who invented those butterfly clips.

Diane was moving back to Colorado to be closer to her family so she was having a going-away party. I was trying to find someone to ride with since I had never been to the bar that was hosting the party.

"Are you going to Diane's party?" I asked.

"I don't know. I haven't decided yet."

As Paige answered, she began to gracefully run her fingers through her long, blond locks like a harpist combing through a classical song.

"I think I'll drop by for a minute."

"What are you wearing? I heard it's a classy bar."

As she asked, she began to pull her silky, straight tresses away from her neck. She continued to maneuver each thin strand into a knot until most of them formed a loose, messy ball.

"Probably some jeans and a dressy shirt," I replied. "Oh, maybe my green one that I wore to your thing a couple of weeks ago."

"That'll be cute. You look great in green. I don't know. What do you think I should wear?"

As she contemplated her outfit, she began to comb her fingers through her loose bun and shake her head to release the strands that she hadn't already freed with her fingers.

"What about your new blue shirt?" I asked.

"I don't know. I think it makes me look fat."

As she imagined herself in her blue shirt, she began to gather her wild hair together and twist the straight strands up toward the top of her head. She took out a black butterfly clip from her desk and clasped the clip to her thick ball of hair.

"You're silly! First of all, if you're fat, then I'm a blimp. And I know that I'm not a blimp. It's just a small party. It's really no big deal."

"You're right. I'm sure I can find something in my closet."

As she assured herself, she removed the clip from her gathered tresses and again shook her long locks loose.

"So, I guess I'll go."
"Okay. Can I ride with you?"
"Sure, I'll see you later."

As she said good-bye she ran both of hands back through her wispy locks to remove the wild hairs out of her face.

Why does this bother me? Why do I care what Paige chooses to do with her hair? I mean it is "her" hair. If I had long, silky hair, maybe I would do the same thing. Okay, maybe not. But do I have a right to be annoyed? It seems that since my roach problem, a lot of things, especially the little things have started to bug me. Adam's sorry apology didn't help either. Their habits have suddenly transformed from an acceptable little souvenir bell to a wind chime in a cold, windy winter. And the consistent ringing has become annoying as hell. Do I have a valid noise complaint? Had I let them infect me with their disease that's immune to different?

Why should I expect them to brush out their habits, and why should I be expected to wash out mine? Sometimes old habits are hard to break. Look how long it took television to break the bad habit of highlighting minority programming with stereotypical streaks before Cosby. Some things just take time. And other things are just meant to remain the same regardless of who is bothered by them. That's just the style of being different. And once we shampoo our egos and condition our minds to accept different for nothing less, maybe we will then be able to get rid of the annoying flakes of dandruff.

domino!

March 9

Dear Diary,

What is it that makes us unique?

1. Color
2. Hair
3. Hips
4. Lips
5. Booty

Maybe it's our way of turning something that is obviously inappropriate into something that seems like it's the right thing to do. Or it could be inner and outer beauty. Then again, it could be our knack for entertaining. We always know how to have a good time regardless of a restricted situation; we can create an enjoyable party anywhere, even in the middle of misery. Some of my most enjoyable family gatherings took place in the midst of mourning. What about loyalty? Or maybe it's confidence. We don't give a damn what anyone thinks. We're going to do what we want when we want to do it and wish that someone would say anything about it. I know that there's not a single right answer to explain our uniqueness but today, I witnessed at least a couple of them.

As soon as I stepped onto the lunch patio, I heard that familiar sound. I could recognize it like a seasoned thief could recognize a fresh victim. But it couldn't be what I thought it was because I was at work, not at Cousin Pookey's house. Maybe I was just imagining things. But my suspicion was quickly proven to be fact.

"Domino, fool!"

No, they didn't! I know these fools were not playing dominoes at work. Where was the opera trio now 'cause this was ghet-to! Didn't they have an errand to run or lunch to eat? Weren't they hungry for something other than the processed food that they had grown up eating? I mean, they had their choice of a buffet filled with quality meats, healthy vegetables, and gourmet desserts. But they were content with their thick cheese and powdered milk.

They were all there: FUBU, Sean John, Phat Farm, Nike, and the one white guy who was willing to give up everything (well, except his job title, family, trust fund, new BMW, and extravagant lifestyle) to be down with the brothas for an hour. But other than that, he just wanted to be considered as one of the homies.

"Hey Racey, you wanna join the game?" Sean screamed from across the way.

adulthood in black

Did y'all forget that we're at work?

But the people on the south side didn't care. They were all about keeping it real! I guess you can't fault them for that but isn't there a time when you have to fake it just a little bit? I mean, I wasn't saying to forget the freedom marches and the equality sit-ins but couldn't they stop the unnecessary looting of inapt behavior that resulted from present riots. What would they think seeing a bunch of black people playing dominoes during lunch? Would they ever promote a domino player who was striving to get twenty-five percent instead of the full one hundred percent? But my brothers didn't care about titles. They were important because of who they were, not because of what title they held.

"No, I'm cool. You guys go ahead with your game."

"You sure? 'Cause Sean's gonna have to get up in a minute anyway," Darren yelled.

"Forget you, man. You just got lucky," Sean replied.

"What you talking 'bout fool? Don't hate 'cause I got game!"

"So you got game?" Sean asked.

"Yeah, I got game."

"You sure 'bout that?"

"Indubitably."

"Spell it," Sean demanded.

"What? Just because you don't know what it means don't mean it's not a word. But don't worry about that, you just need to worry 'bout this."

SLAM!

"Domino! Can you spell that, fool?" Darren shouted.

"You guys are dope," the white guy exclaimed.

For a second we were all confused. We had to go way back to remember what he meant because we hadn't used that word in years. And then the game continued.

"One more game," Sean shouted.

Can y'all spell *appropriate*? What about *professional*? Or *ghetto*? I understand showing your true colors but sometimes you have to cover certain spots so you don't get burned. But they didn't care about sunscreen because they were used to getting burned by stereotypical thoughts anyway. So, the way they looked at it was, stick with what you know and you have better odds of winning.

Now that I think about it, it actually makes me smile a little bit.

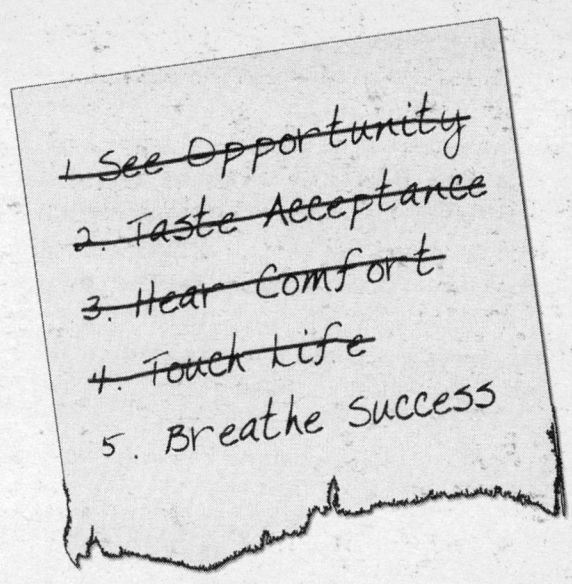

black adulthood

March 23

Dear Diary,

Why is there always traffic? We all have made the mistake of thinking our desired destination is a straight shot—a hop, skip, and a jump away; therefore, never planning for construction. But it seems that just when you think you have finally found an easy street, you are once again detoured to another rough, bumpy road. And suddenly, you begin to feel like this will be the one that will finally destroy your worn alignment. For some reason, it's impossible for us to envision the finished road of success when we're constantly driving down unpaved streets. You find yourself always focusing on the constant congestion of unexpected situations and the traffic delays of your planned dreams. It begins to seem like construction is a never-ending project that will continue to drill into your desired path.

My extended family soon recognized my adulthood in black. I guess they felt that they had done their job raising a model citizen and were ready to treat me like an adult. I am finally allowed to sit at the adult table so I can witness and learn how they behave and interact with each other. But after years of wishing to be like them, I desire to be that free kid again. At least that way, I can sit at a separate table and don't have to witness their annoying, presumptuous behavior. I am suddenly becoming aggravated at the little things that have been a part of the family for generations. I guess I'm beginning to notice every little difference as a result of their different behavior toward me.

Since I am the "new grown-up," I am still treated like a colored adolescence. They assume that my job is to listen, learn, and not contribute to adult conversation. I don't know if they feel threatened by my independence or if they have become accustomed to seeing me as something less. I am still overlooked like I am an invisible Negro child. I am, for the most part, ignored unless I have something they feel is entertaining or satisfying to their simple standards. But now, I am on their level and that isn't a good thing in their eyes. For the first time, they see my intelligence and ambition up close because I am finally tall enough to look them straight in the eye.

After watching them play dominoes the other week, my folks on the south side turned on the light switch to my darkness. I had criticized them for their difference

adulthood in black

but they were happy. Maybe they felt they couldn't win, even if they tried to learn the game of politics. Or maybe their priority wasn't the game itself, but whether they would enjoy playing it. And why should they change their game anyway? If it was working for them, then nothing else mattered, right? It was their free time, and they could do whatever they pleased. Why should they give up who they are? And why should they be forced to play a game that they weren't going to enjoy learning and definitely were going to hate playing, if they didn't refuse first. Everyone has choices. And thanks to my real family, I realized that the only choice that makes sense is myself. I've decided to stop trying to fit into their world and make them fit into mine.

A SENIOR
African-American

african-american senior

March 27

Dear Diary,

Life is too short, and death is too long. There comes a point when we have to stop stirring in grudges and marinating on decisions. We just have to accept the plate that is put in front of us and enjoy it as if it were a home-cooked holiday feast. Life lessons, both good and bad, are the baster for all of the ingredients of our daily nourishment of living. Without experiences, there would be no recipe, and without a recipe there would be no births. And all births, regardless of their features, are born for a purpose. And all life, regardless of their years, eventually die with purpose.

I have never looked forward to growing old. I mean, who wants to experience hair loss and memory lapses? I always thought that it must be terrible to have to depend on people to do things that you once enjoyed doing independently. Imagine suffering from various ailments as a result of different habits and experiences encountered throughout enjoyable years. When I was a teenager, I remember dreading the times when I had to hold Aunt Margaret's aged hand while walking with her because she needed support. I was always embarrassed because here I was stuck with a tired, old woman who walked as slow as an injured snail. But now that I've experienced life, my perception has changed. I now realize the strength of her fingerprint and wish that I could grasp her hand one more time. I now see how that same strength carried me during the longer walks of my journey. I now understand how years spent sprinting for change and progress can create tired, worn feet that must rest sometimes. I finally know why people continue to look forward to the sweet and satisfying taste of desserts at the end of a heavy, satisfying meal.

    Let's face it, we have all created our own perceptions of things we don't know. Opinions are the easy way out; they take the work out of researching and digging up facts. The problem is that all people rely on past opinions to create their personal present-day perceptions. If a pretty girl doesn't speak, regardless if she heard you or not, she is branded stuck-up. If a calm pit bull barks, regardless if the target is an intruder, it is labeled as vicious. If an African-American is introduced into a white workplace, regardless of his background, he is seen, at one point, as the perceptions created from history.

hoodish tendencies

April 7

Dear Diary,

Some things never change. Winter will always produce winds and rain. Spring will always give birth to beautiful flowers and clear skies. Summer will always generate heat and fun. Fall will always display changing colors and scary costumes. And a child born in the hood will always possess "hoodish tendencies." No matter how hard we try to bury our ghetto ways in the sand, the tide always washes them back into our minds. Not that it's always a bad thing. Sometimes they force us to release these inclinations. And other times it's just convenient for us to prosper from our hoodish actions.

Today was a busy day. I had a lot of personal crap to

deal with because of my upcoming weekend. I had moved from an entry-level employee to a manager making just above entry-level pay. My coworkers believed that the promotion was not because of my knowledge or skills; they were sure that the only reason I was picked over them was because of my color. That was fine with me. How many times had one of their own been promoted because they were white? I was also the highest-paid manager because unlike the rest of the pseudo-managers, I had fought and demanded a raise with my new responsibilities.

I had to work both Saturday and Sunday (paid, of course, even though I was the only one who had worked that deal too); therefore, I felt I was fully justified for doing what I would have done this weekend on company time today. Okay, I probably wouldn't have bought the office supplies that I was using for my book club and sorority meeting invitations, but I would have . . . who am I kidding? Even if I had a three-day weekend, I would still be taking care of my personal business at work today. Hey, they owed me! A little paper and copying would not affect the millions of dollars that the company pulled in last year. And I know that I'm underpaid when you compare my hard work to the vice presidents so they owed me these office supplies and a lot more. They better be glad that I wasn't complaining about the "lot more."

In the middle of designing the book club invitation, the phone rang.

"Hello."

"Hey, girl, what you doing?" my best friend from back home, Jackie, asked on the other end of the line. She always called me at work because she could call the company's toll-free number and didn't have to pay a dime.

"Working."

"I need you to do me a favor."

"What?" I asked.

senior african-american

"Can you call Damon?"

Why did I ever call our childhood friend Damon on three-way with Jackie on the phone at work? It was the day that we were talking about Janet Jackson's weight fluxes over the years and we couldn't remember the name of her character on *Fame*. She had insisted it was Penny but I finally convinced her that that was *Good Times*. We knew that Damon would know because he knew *everything* about Janet. That's when she discovered that long-distance calls were on the company. *Hookup!*

I hesitated. "What's the number?"

I was finishing up the last of my book club invites when I noticed that the red light on my second line was still flashing. Damn! What were they talking about? Didn't they know that this was a long-distance call? What reason would I have to call Chicago, if someone decided to pay attention to the phone bill next month? They were taking "hook-up" to another level so I picked up the phone.

"Yeah, *Soul Train* definitely has changed," Damon agreed. "There are more white dancers than black. What happened to the soul?"

See, this is why you can't be nice to people.

"Look, y'all have been on this phone for twenty minutes," I reminded them.

"Has it really been twenty minutes?" asked a surprised Damon.

"Yes, Damon, according to the phone, it's now twenty-three," I noted.

Jackie jumped in, "Why are you trippin', girl? You're not paying for it."

"Look, I have to go, which means, y'all have to get off the phone."

"Oh, okay. Y'all call me next week," Damon said.

"Okay, bye," I said before disconnecting him.

"Bye, Damon. Girl, what you been up to?"

"Nothing, just trying to send out my book club invites today. I'm going to put our last book that I was telling you about in the mail today, so you should have it by tomorrow."

Yes, I was also using the company's mail service. But remember, they owe me.

Why can't we lose these tendencies when we leave the hood? No matter how proper we talk or how much money we make, some "hoodish tendencies" refuse to disappear. And just when you think you have found the antidote to get rid of them, such as a quaint, classy condo, something happens that causes them to resurface again. Maybe there's not a cure because there's nothing wrong with keeping true to who you are and where you come from, even though you're now experiencing the symptoms of success. Some things are just genetic.

Anyway, why should we be expected to just change overnight? And why should we have to change in the first place? Everyone likes free things. It's just when we do it, it's stealing or a hookup. When they do it, it's using their resources and networking. When they do it, they get caught because of their big mouth. When we do it, after it's done, it's over. It's time to move on to the next hookup. It was a waste of time to worry whether or not I was going to get caught. Anyway, I wish they would confront me on a pack of paper and some funky copies. Then I would really act a fool! And the last thing they wanted to do was witness my "hoodish" attitude.

After I sent out the last invitation and restocked my home medicine cabinet with the samples in the company's first aid kit, I was done with another busy day at the office. As I was putting the office supplies back in the supply room, I realized that I had forgotten to finish a report that I

senior african-american

was working on because I'm not going in tomorrow. Since I hadn't called enough in advance, the salon couldn't fit me in next weekend. My only other choice was an appointment tomorrow because she had a cancellation. If not, I'll have to wait another three weeks and I don't have that many hats. So see, I have no other choice. I have to call in sick tomorrow. What? They'll live.

we're not that close!

April 25

Dear Diary,

Don't you hate awkward situations? It doesn't matter if you're the recipient or the presenter of the uncomfortable award; the acceptance speech is never filled with excitement and gratitude. You don't know whether to be ungrateful for the attention or thankful for the honesty. You can't decide whether to be frightened at the moment or relieved that it's over. The whole situation is just . . . how can I say this . . . awkward. But we've all had it happen at least one, especially if you're a minority in a majority workplace. It makes you nauseous just thinking about some of them.

"Another round for everybody!"
I was once again out on the town with some co-

workers after work. And as usual, Craig and Derek both refused to join us. I totally understood because they were still adolescents in their world. But I'm getting too old to hold grudges. If I held a grudge for every little thing that these people have said, done, or implied, I would be seriously overweight with crap that just isn't good for my heart. So, I've decided instead to exercise my mind and only digest healthy thoughts, even if I'm tempted to harbor those that are not good for me. Believe me, it's not easy, and I'm taking it one day at a time. But it's amazing what a little workout regimen can do to you. Once you start lifting weight off your shoulders and crunching negativity on a regular basis, you build strong muscle and the unwanted pounds just melt away.

". . . Get it?" asked Miranda.

Everyone began to laugh at her corny joke. Hey, we were all having a good time—blowing off steam, shooting the breeze, having a few drinks, telling a few jokes—just harmless fun.

"Oh, I have one. I have one," Jeff said.

Okay, he had probably had one too many margaritas. But he was alright, I guess. He was fun, respectful (except to his mother), honest—just an all-around good guy.

"My father-in-law told me this one," he started. "Wait . . . let me think of how it goes . . . Oh, I remember. What is the worst thing you can call a black man that starts with an 'n' and ends with an 'r'?"

Hell, no! I don't care if he had a case of tequila and ate the worm. They never get a free workout pass to exercise that word. I don't care what excuses they give for not being in shape with political correctness.

Just because JaRule's dumb ass wrote it for J-Lo doesn't mean all of us are ignorant enough to give trial memberships to our exclusive vocabulary—and I dare anyone to entertain his ignorant ass with a "what?"

Some quickly sobered up and prepared for my response. Because they knew by now I was going to have *something* to say. And the others were just as oblivious as his stupid butt and anticipated the punch line.

"What?" Amy yelled.

Hell freakin' no!

"A neighbor!" he shouted.

Oh, okay, so it wasn't "the word," but still...

Few started to laugh. Others began to occupy themselves with a drink. And Paige even excused herself from the entire situation by going to the rest room. I don't know why I'm surprised. If he doesn't respect his mama, why would he respect me?

"I really didn't find that funny at all," I asserted.

There was complete silence. It was as if everyone was paying their respects to Amadou Diallo. It had been the same type of jokes that had produced the beliefs of the four men who assumed that all of us have a hidden agenda other than that of exercising our freedom to stand in front of our home.

"Come on, don't be so sensitive. I thought you were cool. It was just a joke," Jeff cried.

Oh! So, I guess that's what Rodney King was after he got his ass beaten—sensitive. Oh, the punches weren't that hard; he was just being too sensitive. You know he did actually begin the high-speed chase, what did you expect; those rioters were being overly sensitive. Give me a break!

"I don't think I'm being sensitive or not cool. It's a matter of what's appropriate and what is not or what's respectful and what is disrespectful. Would you laugh at any jokes that attacked you or your race?" I asked.

"But you know I didn't mean anything by it. It was just a joke."

We are not that close to be telling race jokes.

"There are some things you just don't joke about, and something like that is one of them."

"But you know I'm not like that. I don't understand why you are so offended. I wasn't talking about you."

Oooh! So, it's okay because you were talking about Uncle Sonny or Cousin Pookey.

"Oh, so you were talking about one black man?" I asked.

"But it's not like I was talking about them in particular," he interrupted.

"Look, I think we are blowing this out of proportion," Miranda interjected.

And of course I had to release a little attitude with a neck roll. "I don't think so. There are just some things—I don't care how cool you think we are—that are not allowed in my presence. And that joke or any other joke similar to it falls in that category."

"What can I say? I apologize if I offended you."

Do they think that "I apologize" or "I'm sorry" makes it all better? How many times have I heard "I'm sorry"?

senior african-american

> I'm sorry... I didn't mean it like that...
> I'm sorry, we decided to go with someone more qualified.
> I apologize for my friend. He's a little insensitive.
> I'm sorry for my ancestors' behavior.
> I'm sorry, did that offend you?
> I'm sorry, did you want that fried?

Do they believe that they are justified in telling a joke or pulling over someone who they think can't afford an expensive car or shooting a suspicious-looking man because when it's all said and done, they can rub apologies over the wound and bandage it up to make it all better? Do they really believe that simple words completely heal the cuts of injustice and humiliation?

Don't they know by now that you cannot play with black folks about certain things regardless of who you think you are or what type of sense of humor you think we have? We do not do race jokes. Call us sensitive, uptight, touchy, delicate, but do not—I repeat, do not—call us out of our name or play like you're about to call us out of our name. I had seen them joke around other minority groups, and sure, everyone, including the minorities, laughed at the stereotypical jokes. But black folks don't play like that. And they wonder why they get beat down sometimes.

i don't have twenty on it

June 7

Dear Diary,

Why can't the people in my office fuckin' think for themselves? And why do certain people feel that they're qualified to think for you? I'm so tired of getting e-mails asking and sometimes demanding contributions to a birthday gift or a baby gift or a wedding gift or a going-away gift. The "organizer" never takes the time to find out if you really like the person and if they're worthy of the gift. It's just a mass e-mail to which everyone is expected to adhere. And then they expect you to oblige like you're a child who doesn't know any better. But you can't underestimate all kids, especially the ones with strong parents who have instilled right and wrong in their maturing minds and have taught them to make their own waves instead of going with the flow.

Hello Guys,

We have decided on a farewell gift for Mindy. She really wants to get in shape so we thought a personal trainer would be a great surprise. We got a great deal with an awesome trainer (my boyfriend). I figured if everyone contribute $20, then we could do it! So, please surrender your money no later than Friday. Thanks!

Has Lisa lost her freakin' mind? Can you believe this e-mail? First of all, I don't know Mindy like that. And that is definitely a gift for a friend. I didn't even spend twenty dollars on Paige's Christmas gift and I "like" her. So, what makes anyone think that I would gladly give her twenty dollars for a personal trainer when I'm working out at The Sports Center?

So, Lisa claims that she has figured out all the details. Did she also figure out that Mindy has barely spoken to me for the entire time that I've been here? Or why hasn't she figured out all the work that Mindy *hasn't* done? She owed us a training session or two! Was I the only one who had a problem with this?

"Y'all are not going to give Lisa any money for Mindy's gift, are y'all?" I asked Craig and Derek in a corner.

"Hell, no," Craig answered.

"Not a dime," Derek confirmed.

I knew I could depend on my brothas to do the right thing, but I wasn't so sure about the rest of them.

"Are you going to give twenty dollars for Mindy's gift?" I asked Peter.

I wasn't being messy. I knew he didn't like her

senior african-american

either and I was just trying to see... Okay, I was stirring the pot a little bit.

"I don't want to but I don't have a choice."

What did he mean he didn't have a choice? He had chosen to wear a pastel pink shirt . (Don't you hate to see men in pink?) He had chosen to hate Mindy. He had also chosen to tell me the details of every time she had pissed him off. I thought we all had choices. Wasn't that the purpose of the constitution: freedom of speech, freedom of religion, freedom to not support a ridiculous gift idea for a person you don't even like.

"What do you mean you have no choice?" I asked.

"If I don't give the money, then I'll look bad. And everyone will talk about how I didn't pitch in for the gift and wasn't a team player."

"Well, I don't remember the team voting Lisa the leader so she could decide on a gift that funds her boyfriend's business."

"Yeah, it sucks," he admitted.

"If it sucks, then why are you going to do it?"

"Because when it comes time for a promotion, the person who didn't give twenty dollars to Adam's niece won't be on the list. You know politics."

"So you're saying that you're giving twenty . . . or forget the money. You're giving a gift to someone you don't like because you want to be promoted?"

"Yep!"

Why was I not feelin' this? I was a regular player in the games of success. But this game was like checkers. The rules were changing with every opponent. How could he be comfortable with someone moving for him without discussing it with him first? How could he sacrifice what's right for one move? How could he feel like a winner when he wasn't even involved in the game? And how could he let an amateur like Lisa tell him how to play?

"What about the fact that this is a ridiculous gift that they are demanding we give? We didn't even give a gift to Diane when she left!" I reminded him.

"I know. But what are you going to do, right?"

Let's try thinking for yourself.

"Well, I know that I'm not giving her twenty dollars. And I wish that Lisa would say something."

"Well, good luck."

How were these people going to be leaders when they couldn't even lead themselves to follow their minds? Had they not been taught to think for themselves? Did they not know that having someone insignificant not like you because you didn't buy their friend a gift wasn't going to kill you? Had they not realized that words couldn't hurt you but following someone off a cliff could flatten every dream of success? These followers were more loyal to the game than they were to themselves.

For those of you who have not given me your money, please do so by Friday.
Lisa

Now I'm confused. Why was she sending me another e-mail? Did I tell her that I was going to contribute? Had I replied to her first e-mail telling her that I was going to pitch in for the gift?

Lisa,
Because you have the nerve to send me another e-mail asking me for "anything," I feel the need to be frank. Take me off the fuckin' e-mail list for this and any contribution in the future for any birthdays, baby showers, operations, weddings, or moving-

on gifts. I don't like anyone here enough to even sign my name to a card. And I must note that all I got for my birthday was a grocery store cake. So, if you're waiting on my $20 to buy Mindy a year of training, then she will never get rid of her double chin and fat thighs because I'm not giving a penny!

Okay, so you know I didn't send it. I'm not that stupid! I wasn't going to let them disqualify me that easy. They had to beat me fair and square. I had my own strategy and they had their "one." But what they had failed to realize is that there is more than one strategy in the game of checkers and eventually they were going to have to crown the black one.

but he's black!

June 10

Dear Diary,

Some people are destined to be together.

1. Ossie and Ruby Dee
2. Bill and Camille
3. Will and Jada
4. Magic and Cookie
5. Kermit and Miss Piggy
6. Whitney and Bobby

Then there are those only meant to cross paths. And then there are other people destined to remain distant strangers for a lifetime. Why do people insist on ignoring fate? Why are they so quick to fix you up with a cute friend or a shy cousin or a wealthy neighbor? Do I look like I shouldn't be alone? And why do these people refuse to realize if they wouldn't date them, then chances are I probably wouldn't either, regardless of what we have in common. Do I look that desperate?

"I want to talk to you about something when you have a chance."

That's funny. Mindy had never really talked to me before today. Was she trying to suck up to me for a contribution to her gift?

"What's wrong?"

"Oh, nothing's wrong! I was just wondering, uh, if you're seeing anyone?" she asked.

Okay, I don't even get down like that.

"Why?"

"Normally, I don't do this, but I know this guy who would be perfect for you."

"Why do you think he would be perfect for me?" I asked.

"You guys just look like you belong together. He's smart, attractive, and has a good job."

"Then why is he single?"

"He's a little shy and he doesn't really go out. He just moved here like six months ago," she explained.

"How do you know him?"

"Oh, he's my neighbor. So you're single, right?"

"How do you know?"

"Because I was telling Lisa about you two and she

senior african-american

told me. Look, you should really meet him. You guys would be so cute together," she insisted.

"Uh, I don't know. What does he look like?"

"He is fine, girlfriend! And he has really smooth skin."

"Really?"

"Look, what if we do a drinks thing with a group, you know, very informal? If you don't like him then you're not forced to talk to him all night."

"Oh, alright. What do I have to lose, right?"

"Right. But I'm telling you, you're going to really like him."

I don't know why, but I agreed to do this love-connection thing. What did I have to lose, right? She said that he was fine and had great skin so he must be tolerable on the eyes. But why was she doing this? She barely spoke to me and when she did, it was just "hello." What did she have to gain? Was she getting something out of this matchmaking scheme?

A week had passed and Mindy was still overly excited about hooking me up with her friend. I have to admit, as I walked in the bar, I was a little nervous about meeting Mr. Right.

"He's not here yet," she said when I arrived.

"Okay, I'll just get a drink. I'll be back."

I was relieved because I hadn't seen anyone who caught my eye as I did a quick scan of the bar. So far, so good. I started to have a good feeling about this. Maybe she really knew fate. And maybe she had an idea of what I was and wasn't looking for in a guy. I began to wonder if maybe this was my year. I was going to find Mr. Right and get married and then have two kids, a boy and a girl. It was finally my time! I had a feeling. Maybe it was the same feeling that she had gotten and that's why she was hooking us up in the first place. See, they're not all bad.

So, I spoke too soon again. I knew who he was as soon as his ugly butt disrupted the "I'm single and I like to mingle" vibe of the bar. At that point, we were the only two black people in the place. It wasn't rocket science. At first I was mad at him for looking like he had just stepped off a video shoot in the dirty south and was now on his way in his tight black leather pants to do a fashion shoot for Leather R Us. I bet he had a good job. The question was, Was it legal? Because of his nonstop, Chester-the-cat grin, his mouthful of platinum was shining brighter than the sun on a bright, sunny day. Maybe that was it. Maybe Mindy had never seen how he really looked because his teeth always blocked her view. But clearly she should have seen his unshaven face or his unkempt dreads or both of his tattooed arms. Had someone told him that the Tasmanian devil was cute? And that was just one of the many ridiculous pieces of art that he was wearing on his arms. Oh, and let's not talk about what he was wearing—or shall I say wasn't wearing. No socks. No lotion. No class. Do I even have to continue? I know you get the idea. Surely, we didn't even belong in same bar.

But then I got in touch with my anger and directed it to the real culprit. I know she didn't! Perfect couple my ass! What was she smokin'? Or by looking at him, what were they smokin'? Could she really see me with this guy? Could she really see him? Because if she had, then the answer to my first question most definitely would have been "no."

"So, what do you think?" she asked excitedly.

I was speechless. The only thing I could say was . . .

"What the hell? Uh, no."

"But can't you at least say hello," she begged.

"Uh, no. Look, I have to go."

senior african-american

"But you guys are so much alike."

So, that was it! I finally solved the puzzle. Everything started to make sense. We were *alike*. Well, clearly there was only one thing that was *alike* when it came to him and me.

What she meant to say was, "But he's black!"

They never make it hard for you to dissect their dysfunctional brains, do they? It's always so obvious to tell what they are thinking and why. So, she had met another black person and immediately a bell went off in her head. The only two black people I know are meant to be together!

"Would you date him?" I asked.

Suddenly, she had nothing to say.

"Tell me, would you date him?" I asked her again.

"I don't know. I've never really looked at him in that way."

What she meant to say was, "Hell no! My parents would kill me."

"Yeah, it doesn't look like you've looked at him at all."

"You can't tell me that he doesn't have a great body."

"Well, I can't tell with all of the tattoos covering it."

"He's an artist."

"I thought you said he had a good job."

"He does. He's a salesman but he's an artist on the side."

"What does he sell, platinum teeth?"

"No, actually he's into real estate. But you should see his art. It's so beautiful and inspiring. I've never seen anything like it."

"Yeah, I know what you mean. Look, this is not a good idea."

"What's wrong? He isn't your type?"

What she meant to say was, "But he's black!"

It was my time all right . . . it was my time to go. That's what my butt got for thinking too far ahead. Before I even passed him on my way out, I caught a whiff of the combination of his cheap cologne and dirty dreads. I suddenly became infuriated. How could she play me like that? And how could I not know that I was getting played? But why am I not surprised? Thinking back, how could she have possibly known that we would make a good couple? She didn't even know me. I had never even held a conversation with her until the day that she proposed that I meet the funky, tight-shirt–wearing artist. She didn't know my likes and dislikes. She didn't even know what I was looking for in a man. So, how could she call herself finding my Mr. Right when she didn't even know what my Mr. Wrong looked like? And they wonder why we don't trust them sometimes.

are you talking to me?

June 23

Dear Diary,

I wonder what it's like to stand without a backbone. Is it even possible? One would think that you have to have some type of support to keep your head up. I know sometimes it's hard. We are often tempted to stare at our feet due to all of the crap that lies in front of our paths. But some of us have been forced to learn how to multitask as we walk. We have become accustomed to walking over puddles without even looking down. But it's not an art that you can just pick up after a few lessons. It's like playing the piano. I mean, anyone can bang out notes, but everyone can't create music without staring at the ivory keys.

"What are you, fucking stupid! How could you buy

fucking nuts when you know I'm allergic to them? How many times do I have to say it for you to get it through your tiny brain! . . . And what's this? Where did you get this rotten-ass fruit? It doesn't look fresh enough. Didn't I tell you that I only wanted fruit from Whole Foods? God, this is fucking unacceptable!"

As one would have guessed by now, the recipient of Adam's verbal abuse wasn't one of us. Why? Our forefathers had no choice but to take crap like this, but now we are free . . . free to kick anybody's ass who'd dare to speak to us with any of those disrespectful syllables. With all of the past cruelty toward our people, there's no way in hell that we would ever allow anyone to even attempt to treat us like unwanted stepchildren. People better recognize! If that would have been me, it would have went something like this . . . Rewind please.

"!elbatpeccanu gnikcuf si siht ,doG ?sdooF elohW morf tiurf detnaw ylno I that uoy llet I t'ndiD .hguone hserf kool t'nseod tI ?tiurf ssa-nettor siht teg uoy did erehW ?siht si tahw dnA . . . !niarb ynit ruoy hguorht ti teg ot uoy rof ti yas ot evah I od semit ynam woh ?meht ot cigrella m'I wonk uoy nehw stun gnikcuf yub uoy dluoc woH !diputs gnikcuf ,uoy era tahW"

He would have started out with, "What are you, fucking stupid . . . "

And I would I responded with, "I'm sorry, are you talking to me?"

"What?"

"I was wondering if you thought you were talking to me in *that* tone? You know what? I'm just going to let you cool down and then you can come and talk to me when you're ready. How about that?"

And with that, the only thing he would have been talking to would have been my voluptuous behind. What's wrong with people? People have lost their freakin'

senior african-american

minds! How can anyone even think of talking to anyone that way? If it were a child, he could even cry child abuse. And we are talking about adults—grown-ass people! Are people that desperate for a job? Do they not know that jobs are everywhere and just like they got one, they could get another one? Where's self-respect? Where's self-confidence? Where's common sense?

"Did you hear how he just yelled at me?" Amy asked.

Yeah, and I also heard how you just allowed him to yell at you.

"Yeah, I heard."

"He's such an asshole. Last week he screamed at me because there weren't any nuts in his kitchen. And this week, he's allergic. Can he make up his fuckin' mind? I hate this job. It's like I'm his personal slave."

Oh, so now you see how it feels—not so fun, is it?

Of course, this wouldn't be a problem with us. There are just some things we just don't take to: heat, bungee jumping, tanning, swimming (for females with fresh perms), skydiving, raves, hockey, golf (if Tiger isn't playing), bluegrass, and oh yeah, any form of disrespect.

Moments later, Adam returned to Amy's desk.

"Racey, is it possible for me to get another copy of the quarterly report? Some pages came out too light for me to read."

"Sure, Adam," I replied.

Usually they know. They know the difference between the ones who they can step over and those who they have to walk around.

"And Amy, why do I have a goddamn meeting set for six-thirty tonight? How many times do I have to tell you, no meetings after six?"

"I asked you last week and you said that it was okay," Amy reminded him.

"You should've known that I wasn't paying fucking attention! Cancel it," he yelled.

As he stormed away, I began to wonder how do they separate the wills from the will nots. Is it instinct? Do they just know? I guess you can say that that's one stereotype that works in our favor in the workplace. Because of the militant perceptions, we seldom have to deal with screaming. Or maybe it's just practice. You can learn anything after one costly mistake. After witnessing the horrific effect of feeding a thirsty community a not-guilty verdict of chocolate dump cake, society quickly learned the error of its ways and later quenched the thirst with a cup of OJ to nourish the low-calcium bodies. I guess that's how it works: feed the hungry souls with respect and starve the full stomachs with impudence. See, they're not all clueless.

friend vs. associate

September 13

Friend: *A person whom one knows, likes and trusts*
Associate: *A person united with another or others in an act or business; a partner or colleague*

Dear Diary,

Why do we take words for granted?

"I love you."
"How are you?"
"This is my friend."

These are some of the phrases we use so often that they have slowly turned into habit words without definition. For some reason, people have become accustomed to not needing to think about the true meanings of words before they insert them into their everyday conversation. It's like answering fine to "How are you?" because it's the easier and expected answer. Well, that's true for "some" of us.

I was at lunch with Paige and Peter discussing possible plans for my upcoming birthday.

"Why don't you have a party for your birthday?" Paige asked.

"Well, I don't have that many friends out here. They're all back home," I answered.

"What about us?" Peter asked.

What about y'all?

"Yeah, what are we?" Paige insisted.

I didn't want to answer that question because I knew the consequences, and I just didn't feel like a debate. But I had already made my opening argument, so...

"I wouldn't consider you guys friends per se," I replied.

"What do you mean? I consider you a friend."

"Yeah, me too," Peter agreed.

"I'm just saying that I only have a few friends in this world. A friend is someone you can count on no matter what. Or someone you can tell any and everything. A friend is someone you have been through some stuff with, you know what I mean?"

"No, I don't. So what am I?" Paige pressured.

"Well, I consider you guys, uh, associates."

"Associates?" they both asked in unison.

"Yeah, associates," I confirmed.

"That's all I am, an associate?" Paige asked.

"What? There's nothing wrong with being an associate."

"Well, it's not like it's a friend," Paige explained.

"Wait a minute, guys. Now how can I call you a friend when I don't really know you outside of work? I mean, we've done stuff like dinner and parties but I wouldn't call you and you wouldn't call me if you were in serious trouble."

"But I would totally help you out, if you called," Peter assured.

"Yeah, I would too," Paige agreed.

"I'm not saying you wouldn't. I'm just saying that I wouldn't call in the first place," I said.

"Man, that hurts," Peter confessed.

"Yeah, I really thought we were friends," Paige said.

"Look, you're acting like I'm saying I hate you."

Not all the time anyway.

"I'm just saying that the word *friend* means something to me that it obviously doesn't mean to you. I have a few friends and that's it. These are people that I trust completely, no matter what. And you can't develop that overnight or even in a year."

"Well, associate sounds so formal and work related," Peter said.

That's because you are my coworkers.

"So, what? You guys want a different name?" I asked.

"Yeah, something less formal," Paige suggested.

"Okay, what about *friendlies*. Not quite a friend but more than an associate."

"That sounds better. But you're still my friend," Paige confirmed.

So easily amused.

"Thanks, I guess."

Why is it so important for people to have a large amount of friends? I understand when you're young you need to be liked and understood. You need friends to play games like hopscotch and hide and seek. But as you grow older, there are only a few people from whom you can't hide your true feelings and you feel comfortable seeking their help. When you get to be a certain age, it's not about the number of people who like you but it's about that select group of people you can trust. At a certain point you realize that there are some who will dislike you for whatever reason, and that's okay. And then there are some who just will never understand for other reasons and that also becomes okay.

"This is my pal . . ."
"This is my buddy . . ."
"This is my friend . . ."

It's amazing how some words possess different meanings to different people. I mean, I like Peter and Paige. And Paige is my closest coworker but were we really friends? We had worked with each other for almost two years. We occasionally had lunch together. We had been out to dinner a few times. And we had gone to a festival once. Yep, that was the extent of our time spent together. I know that I could depend on them if I was in trouble. I guess I knew and liked them but could I trust them one hundred percent. Could I trust anyone in this office wholeheartedly? These were the same people who had assumed that a head wrap was a baseball cap and that a unique language was unintelligent. This was the exact group who intruded on my privacy and sang the lyrics of the forbidden songs that they declared feebleminded. These were the same coworkers who had little respect for their mother and less respect for any history besides their own. How could you mix up Martin and Malcolm?

senior african-american

They didn't know my past, so how could they understand my present battles and future obstacles? And even if I explained my strategic plan, there wasn't a guarantee that they would leave their comfortable homes and go to combat with me. So, if I couldn't count on them to fight or even understand my ongoing war, how was I going to trust them enough to be a true friend?

today was a good day
October 27

Dear Diary,

This shit is getting old. I've been here two years and I'm tired. I'm tired of coming here every day looking into their cold, blue eyes. I'm tired of stupid questions and inappropriate responses. I'm tired of the stereotypes. I'm tired of the denial. I'm tired of wannabes and fakers. I'm tired of not being understood for my feelings of loneliness and disgust. I'm tired of being forced to adapt. I'm tired of blond hair and tanned skin. I'm tired of the backstabbers and the foes. I'm tired of the jokes. I'm tired of hearing their phony laughs and forced smiles. I'm tired of feeling like there's something wrong with me. I'm sick and tired of the ignorance and jealousy. I'm tired of different. And I'm tired of feeling guilty for being tired.

After all this time, I've finally had an overdue revelation. It's time to stop worrying over the same bullshit and just let my blackness live, regardless of who doesn't understand it or doesn't prefer it over their own. I refuse to harbor all of the greatness of being Black, Afro-American, African-American, or whatever they're calling us these days.

Say it loud! I'm black and I'm proud!

It seems that the more you try to conceal it and only use it when it's beneficial to you, the more you lose the connection with the brilliance of what it is that makes us different. You begin to think like the majority. You start to put the unique qualities down in order to lift yourself up to what's perceived as their higher level to justify your abandonment of it. But sometimes, we have to reach the top to figure out why black folks don't skydive. We're just better off on the ground. I can now identify with the people on the south side. From now on, I'm not going to think twice about whether I'm using Mother, Mom, or Mama (depending who I'm talking to). I'm not turning my radio down when I'm the designated driver for the carpool to lunch. I'm not doing anything "extra" to try and appease their small-minded asses. If I feel like soul food for lunch, I'm just going to throw out my suggestion along with all the other ones, regardless if people think it's too greasy or heavy for their diet. Forget trying to satisfy their hunger before mine. I'm not going home another day starving and craving to belong in their world.

Normal is never forced to understand different, however, different is always struggling to become normal. Over the years, I've often wondered, why do we continue to aspire to be like them? Who made them the role models? Sure, they have proven that they have good business sense by investing in others' stocks and walking away with the returns, but is that really what we aspire to become, skillful investors? I know that the same labels that left scars on our ancestors' backs are still beating us today. But why can't we just be like us? We're just as great as the next group. We're worth no more or no less. But for some

senior african-american

reason, we're constantly wondering why we have four quarters instead of a single paper bill not understanding that everyone has the same value. And also not realizing that paper tears.

What will it take? Should we just separate ourselves as they have attempted to do in the past? Should we stop taking our differences for granted by accepting anybody who has a little bit of rhythm or proclaim that they're "down" in our exclusive club? Should we stop trying to become them? Should we start celebrating and cherishing our unique contributions instead of just giving them away for four quarters? Why can't we build and put ourselves on an even higher pedestal than we have managed to build for them? Why is it so hard? Why does it seem impossible?

Once again, it has taken growth and time but I have finally accepted different for what it is and what it isn't. And I can finally celebrate who I am. That's why I can't hate. I refuse to envy. And I can finally understand a little bit. No matter how hard we try to blend into society, we will always be "different." It's like a big pot of rustic gumbo. Everyone, out of habit, will always concentrate on the taste of the big chunks of meat instead of recognizing the roux and spices that actually produce the mouthwatering taste. But you can't starve society either. There comes a point where you have to stop blaming the cook, even though he prepares the pot, for bland meals when you have the pepper and salt sitting together right in front of you. It's possible to succeed. It's possible to coexist. It's possible to work together.

I've realized that just like I have carried my family's game plan with me all these years, they are playing with their family's plan, and I can't disqualify them for that. Actually, that's what makes the game interesting. Imagine if we were all playing the same plays in the same uniforms with the same mascot cheering us to victory. Imagine if it was that easy. There will be no game and life will be as boring and predictable as a game of Operation without batteries. There would be no battles. There would also be no victories. So you win some and you lose some. That's just a part of living.

So, what do I want to change? And whom do I want to change exactly? If I fight for change in them then I have to be willing to change myself as well, and I don't know if that's possible. We all harbor perceptions. We all form opinions. We all occupy thoughts. We all play with unwritten rules. Sure, most of the time, they may have home team advantage. And sure they are the authors of the rule book. But that doesn't guarantee victory. Once you figure out that the unwritten rules of perception don't involve a certain college education or a trade to another team, you can accept and understand the game as a whole. And that is what makes you a better player. It gives you a greater advantage of defeating the unexpected attacks, the prejudiced fouls, the stressful time-outs, and the redundant obstacles of the American workplace. And you finally begin to ignore your weariness and gain the strength to recognize the rewarding experiences and small victories of the game.

As you get older, you get wiser and you finally figure out how life works. As I look back on my nigger birth, negro childhood, colored adolescence, and black adulthood, I have seen with my own pretty hazel eyes that nothing is easy, but everything is possible. I finally realize that I only have a certain amount of time to experience life, and I can't spend my last days wishing instead of being. And everything that I've gone through conceives the being. So, I'm not mad at my extended family for their false perceptions. I've even formed lasting relationships with some of my cousins, regardless of our family disagreements.

senior african-american

Family is still family. And they're not all bad. I knew that eventually, they would see me, regardless of whether they wanted to or not, for what I am, an African-American woman. Grant it, it's not fair that I had to constantly fight for my well-earned title, but that's life and life isn't always fair. And once I accepted that, I welcomed a newly formed independence and self-acceptance.

Child, I'm not worried about those folks anymore. I've got my own life, and I refuse to let anyone live it besides me. So, if I don't feel like doing it, I'm not. If I can't do it, I won't. And if I don't believe in doing it, I ain't.

What else has life taught me over these years? There are so many things, I wouldn't even know where to begin. Let's start with faith. Without it, I would have buried my dreams a long time ago. I can't forget desire. That's the only thing that kept me dreaming. And maybe endurance. With that, I survived all of the necessary growing pains. Forgiveness was key to battle the bitterness and pain. And truth . . . let's not forget truth. That was vital in me learning that different doesn't hinder me from growth and achievement but normal can.

What else do I have to say? Oh, yeah, live without regret. I've grown too old to wonder what if or should've, would've, could've. Now, I'm just concentrating on am. I am struggle. I am sacrifice. I am courage. I am minority. I am Raceyneisha. I am frustration. I am progress. I am victory. I am freedom. I am confusion. I am anger. I am impatience. I am hopeful. I am growth. I am human. I am culture. I am beauty. I am unique. I am success. I am talent. I am intelligence. I am strength. I am confidence. I am proud. I am professional. I am wisdom. I am purpose. I am choice. I am past. I am present. I am future. I am proof. I am Nigger. I am Negro. I am Colored. I am Black. I am African-American. I am different. I am equal. I am worthy. I am a Nigger, Negro, Colored, Black, African-American woman.

40 Hours and an Unwritten Rule

1. ~~See Opportunity~~
2. ~~Taste Acceptance~~
3. ~~Hear Comfort~~
4. ~~Touch Life~~
5. ~~Breathe Success~~